# SILKEN Chains

# SILKEN Chains

## BOOK 1

### Bond by Morozov Bratva

**MYA GREY**

Copyright @ 2024 by Mya Grey

All rights reserved.

No part of this book may be reproduced in any form or by any electronic or mechanical means, including information storage and retrieval systems, without written permission from the author, except for the use of brief quotations in a book review.

ASIN: B0CZWTQGMC
IBSN: 9798326308177

# *ACKNOWLEDGEMENT*

*To my darling readers,*

If you're diving into this new series, "*Bond by Morozov Bratva*," you must be craving a love story that's as toxic as it is tantalizing. Well, buckle up, because you're in for a wild ride. Between these pages, you'll find a tale of raw passion, dangerous obsession, and a bond that defies all reason.

But be warned - this isn't your typical romance. Victor Morozov and Laura Ann Thompson are not your average star-crossed lovers. They're complex, flawed, and unapologetically intense. They'll pull you into their dark, seductive world of the Russian Bratva and make you question everything you thought you knew about love.

So, get cozy, pour yourself a stiff drink, and prepare to have your heart raced and your pulse pounded. I promise you a journey you won't soon forget, full of heart-stopping suspense, sizzling chemistry, and the kind of morally ambiguous characters that you can't help but root for.

Remember - in the world of the Bratva, love is a battlefield. It's messy, it's complicated, and it's always a gamble. But when the stakes are this high and the passion is this fierce, it's impossible not to get caught up in the thrill of it all.

*You've been warned.*

Now let's see if you can handle the heat of Victor and Laura's story...

Happy reading, you insatiable romantics.

Mya

# *ALSO BY MYA GREY*

### Bond by Morozov Bratva

Silken Chains (Book 1)
Velvet Chains (Book 2)

### Ivankov Legacy (Standalone) Edition

The Oath of Seduce (Book 1)
The Thorns of Seduce (Book 2)
The Veils of Seduce (Book 3)

### Ivankov Bratva Trilogy

Twisted Seduction (Book 1)
Tangled Seduction (Book 2)
Fateful Seduction (Book 3)

### Brutal Kings Series
*Series I*
*(Dario & Nikki)*
Owned (Book 1)
Craved (Book 2)
Ruled (Book 3)
Possessed (Book 4)
Desired (Book 5)
OR
### Brutal Kings, Series I
(Complete Boxset)

*Series II*
*(Mateo & Andy)*
Dazzle (Book 1)
Charm (Book 2)

Blaze (Book 3)
Flare (Book 4)
Glitter (Book 5)
*OR*
**Brutal Kings, Series II**
(Complete Boxset)

*Series III*
*(Raoul & Emma)*
Captive (Book 1)
Savage (Book 2)
Sinner (Book 3)
Crown (Book 4)
Vow (Book 5)
*OR*
**Brutal Kings, Series III**
(Complete Boxset)

**The Broken Prince Series**
Chased (Book 1)
Seduced (Book 2)
Claimed (Book 3)
Desired (Book 4)
Craved (Book 5)
Loved (Book 6)
*OR*
**The Broken Prince Series Collection**
(Complete Boxset)

# *CONTENT WARNING*

This book contains mature themes and explicit content that may not be suitable for all readers. Please be advised that the following topics are depicted or discussed: graphic violence, self-harm, domestic abuse, sexual situations, emotional abuse, physical abuse, and sexual assault.

Reader discretion is strongly advised.

# TABLE OF CONTENTS

Acknowledgement ................................................................... v
Also by Mya Grey.................................................................. vii
Content Warning .................................................................... ix
Prologue ..................................................................................1
Chapter 1 ................................................................................5
Chapter 2 ..............................................................................13
Chapter 3 ..............................................................................21
Chapter 4 ..............................................................................28
Chapter 5 ..............................................................................35
Chapter 6 ..............................................................................44
Chapter 7 ..............................................................................49
Chapter 8 ..............................................................................54
Chapter 9 ..............................................................................59
Chapter 10 ............................................................................65
Chapter 11 ............................................................................75
Chapter 12 ............................................................................84
Chapter 13 ............................................................................92
Chapter 14 ..........................................................................101
Chapter 15 ..........................................................................108
Chapter 16 ..........................................................................118
Chapter 17 ..........................................................................125
Chapter 18 ..........................................................................132
Chapter 19 ..........................................................................139
Chapter 20 ..........................................................................148
Chapter 21 ..........................................................................154

| | |
|---|---|
| Chapter 22 | 159 |
| Chapter 23 | 163 |
| Chapter 24 | 174 |
| Chapter 25 | 183 |
| Chapter 26 | 190 |
| Chapter 27 | 196 |
| Chapter 28 | 203 |
| Chapter 29 | 210 |
| Chapter 30 | 216 |
| Chapter 31 | 226 |
| Chapter 32 | 233 |
| Chapter 33 | 241 |

# Prologue

*Laura*

"**GET YOUR** fucking hands off my woman," thunders a voice from the depths of somewhere between hell and here. Its resounding echo resonates within the scant distance between Mr. Grabby Hands and me.

I, along with Mr. Grabby Hands, snap our heads around toward the voice that threatens to pull the earth from under our feet. Standing before us is a man with eyes so stormy, they could put the gray clouds above to shame. He towers over everyone else, a clear head and shoulders above the rest, dressed in a sleek dark suit that clings just right to his muscled frame. The top button of his crisp white shirt is undone, teasing with a hint of bronzed skin and the beginnings of ink creeping toward his throat. Dark hair frames a face that's all sharp angles, with a jaw that's enhanced by just the right amount of stubble.

Good lord. If my pussy could pack a suitcase, it'd be straddling his face by now.

He is the cliche alpha male from every over-spiced romance novel. With eyes that drill holes right through your conscience. The sort I read about while sipping lukewarm coffee, wrapped up in my below-average life. This can't be real, but here he is, hotter than the flames that consumed my store. Except, this isn't a book; this is my catastrophic, now seemingly fictional reality.

He steps forward, and with each step, the ground seems to resonate with authority. Or perhaps it's just my wildly beating heart echoing in my ears. There's an air of danger about him—and not the kind that comes with not wearing a helmet while riding a bike. No, this is the "I-can-snap-your-neck-if-I-wanted-to" kind of danger.

"F-fuck off!" Mr. Grabby Hands manages to croak out, but he already looks defeated, shrinking two sizes down. Even in my distracted state, I can't miss the ironic humor of the situation. My would-be assailant is now seeking an exit strategy.

"Back off before I make sure those dirty hands can't touch another damn thing. Specially not my woman," he growls.

The world halts—or is that just my brain short-circuiting?

*His woman? Is he referring to me?*

Mr. Stormy-Eyes strides up and now stands right beside me, the distance between us alarmingly minimal. In one fluid motion, he pulls me closer by my waist. Is this guy trying out for some romance novel audition or what? I could shove him away, but then I'd be robbing myself of the closeness to all that well-tailored charm. Maybe I'll let this slide. Because if my pussy had a vote, it'd be a unanimous, "Yes, please, and thank you."

Damnit! Get a grip, Laura. *There's no way this is happening to me, right?*

You see, my life's a blank page waiting for a story that never really starts.

Thirty-two, with an average face, average body, and average existence, dipped in a lackluster marriage. I guess my excitement peaked and plateaued at the spicy love stories that once lined the shelves of my now-charred bookstore. Yup, I am that girl, living vicariously through fictional characters.

But here's the kicker: the newest thief in my life isn't some masked intruder or a conniving husband. *Nope.* It's fire, with a capital F, yanking away every semblance of normalcy I had.

Flashback to earlier today, when the axis of my painfully ordinary world is tipping completely off its hinge. My day begins with the gut-wrenching realization that my cherished haven of books, a sanctuary built through generations of my family, has turned into nothing but ashes and burned remnants of literary worlds once vivid and alive between their covers.

The realization crashes into me: everything is gone, swallowed by ruthless flames that consumed years of hard work and cherished memories.

How do I tell Dad?

The image of his condescending sneer pops into my mind. The same face that always looked at me as if I were the consolation prize because the universe denied him a son. He won't even need to say it... I know.

Laura, you've screwed up. Again.

In the middle of this, I catch the distant jingle of the ice cream truck that usually parks right outside during summer. "Tropical Delight," it advertises in bold, multicolored letters. The jingle sounds almost mocking, given my current predicament. The smell of burned wood assaults my nostrils, a harsh departure from the comforting scent of old books and dust that used to embrace me. I've been robbed of that, too.

I find myself getting robbed quite a lot lately.

Yups.

Robbed. Swindled. Betrayed—all the dramatic verbs you can find in a dictionary—all happening to good old Laura. Hell, if my life were a book right now, it would be a tragicomedy with a sprinkle of crime mystery, and guess who would be the unwitting protagonist?

But let's refocus on Mr. Stormy Eyes, suddenly right next to me, all up in my space. That look he's giving me? It's like he's trying to claim me with just a glare. Which, okay, shouldn't be as hot as it is. But as he tugs me closer, a nagging thought hits. *Hold on... Have I met this dangerously handsome stranger before?*

*Why does he seem so... familiar?*

# Chapter 1

*Victor*

*Three months ago*

**"YOU UNDERSTAND** what that means, don't you, *Dave, David,* or whatever the fuck you call yourself?" My voice is a cold, hard slap in the silence of the warehouse, even over the echoing sound of Misha's open palm colliding with David's flesh again and again.

Tied to a wooden chair, David is rendered helpless, trapped with no way out. David's cheek sports a fresh, blooming red handprint; his lips spit blood with each cruel contact of skin against skin. His whimpering is sickening. But it's the tears, the trembling chin of his that truly irk me.

Weakness has no place in this world he ventured into.

"I-I understand, Victor, I..." he stammers, his voice trembling like the rest of him. But Misha's laughter, an evil soundtrack to David's humiliation, cuts him off.

"Oh, he understands, Victor. He understands he's *fucked*." Misha chortles, his mirth dark and filled with disdain. His next slap is harder, and David's head snaps to the side.

"The forty-eight hours you were given are up, David. And what do we have? Excuses," I spit the words at him, venom dripping from every syllable.

David's futile attempt to compose himself is pathetic. "The market crashed. I-I couldn't do anything. I need more time. Please." His plea is desperate, almost as desperate as the situation he's in.

"The market," I echo, my voice a mocking dagger. "Seems like the market has more balls than you."

I watch David's face crumble. *But really, what the hell did he think would happen?* He snatched the Morozov Bratva's cash, tried playing trader, and botched it. No one is this stupid to think they can get away alive from that.

"You think you're clever, huh, *suka*?" I sneer, my tone dripping with disdain. "Skimming off the top for two years, playing with the Morozov Bratva's money. *My* money! But two million? *Blyad*! Have you lost your fucking mind?"

David's eyes dart frantically, the weight of his betrayal pressing him further into his own grave. His usual confident smirk is now replaced with a trembling lip.

"Victor, please, I thought—"

"You thought?" I cut in, laughing coldly. "You thought you could steal from us, and we wouldn't notice? Should've stuck to your day job as an accountant, you fucking cockroach."

He swallows hard, the prominent gulp visible against the pale canvas of his terrified throat.

"It was a bad trade, Victor. I can fix this."

I step closer, invading his space, making him feel the magnitude of his fuck-up.

"Fix this? You're two million in the hole, *pizdec*. You're going to find out what happens when you cross the Morozov Bratva."

Without warning, my fist shoots out, crashing into David's stomach with enough force to send both him and the chair he's tied to flying backward. The thud echoes in the room, and he wheezes, trying to catch his breath. He spits out blood, his pretty-boy face now distorted, swelling up, making him look like a grotesque parody of his former self.

"Look at you, *blin*. Once a suave little shit, now just a broken, bloody conman," I sneer, looking down at him with disdain.

He's gasping, eyes filled with terror. "Victor, I swear, I can get the money back."

I lean down, letting him see the cold rage in my eyes. "David, you think money is all I want from you? *No*. I want you to understand what it feels like to truly fuck with the Morozov Bratva.

His voice trembles, desperation evident. "Victor, please. I have a plan. Just give me a chance."

I chuckle, the sound dripping with derision. "A chance? Like the one you had with our money? No, *suka*. No more games. You remember Ari?"

I gesture to the shadowy figure standing in the corner. The man steps forward, a wicked blade glinting in his hand. David's eyes widen in recognition and horror.

"Ari specializes in... reminders," I say, my voice laden with malice. "And he's going to give you one you'll never forget."

A sharp whistle slices through the tension. From the dimmest corner of the warehouse, the hulking shadow of Yuri moves closer. I'm a tall guy, six feet five, and tower over most.

*But Ari?*

Even I have to admit that next to him, I feel like a kid looking up at his dad. He's a beast. Every step he takes is calculated; his towering figure looms like a specter.

David gulps, his Adam's apple bobbing nervously. "Wait, Victor... I can give you something else..."

I raise an eyebrow, intrigued despite myself. "Oh? Do tell."

"My *wife*... L-Laura," he stammers. "She owns a bookstore, Thompson Tales on Fifth Ave. It's worth a lot, maybe not enough to cover my debts. but I could... I could sign it over."

I tilt my head, my voice heavy with mock curiosity. "A *wife*? You? Now that's news. I had my guys check every corner of your life. But married with a *wife*?"

David pales, eyes darting. "Listen, it's... I swiped the 'David Garner' identity years ago. Who... who knows where the real guy is? Dead, disappeared, whatever. And Laura she... she thinks—"

Misha doesn't even let David finish, landing a brutal slap across his face.

Another follows.

"Please... no more," David pleads.

I lean in closer, feeling the tremble of his breath against my skin. "So, tell me, Davey-boy. Does *Laura* know she's married to a ghost? That she's pledged herself to an identity that's not even real?"

David's eyes widen in terror. "No, she doesn't know. She believes in us. In the life we have."

I laugh. "Technically, she's not even married, is she? Since David Garner is six feet under somewhere while you parade around in his shoes. And you managed to pull one over on me, huh? That's a first," I sneer.

"No, I didn't mean to—" David's pale face goes a shade paler.

I scoff, genuinely impressed. "You're even slimier than I gave you credit for."

"It's not like that... with Laura," he confirms, voice shaky. "She thinks I'm just an accountant, that I... that I lead a simple life."

Mikhail's smirk widens. "Accounting for the Morozov Bratva and laundering money on the side. Jesus, she landed a real fucking prince, didn't she?"

"So, you played her? Slithered your way into her life, pretended to marry her using a dead man's identity, and kept her clueless about who the real *David* the dickhead really is?" I sneer, my disgust evident. "Now you want to throw her and her bookstore under the bus for your monumental fuck-ups?"

His voice wavers, almost a whisper. "It wasn't meant to go this way. Everything just... went to shit."

*Who the fuck is this guy?*

David, or whatever his real name is, this sneaky conman, had used another identity for everything.

"And she's worth... *what*, two fucking million?" I sneer, circling him slowly like a shark circling its prey before grabbing him by his bloody shirt.

David tries to muster some semblance of dignity, his voice a raspy plea. "It's a start, Victor. Please. Let me make it right."

I step back, releasing him. "So, you want me to have your wife and think that all will be forgiven." I snort. "She must be something else." I give a mocking whistle.

David's eyes dart, searching for any sliver of mercy. "That's all I have for now. The bookstore's profitable, and... and she can offer... *other things*."

"*Other things?*" My voice is a dangerous snarl, my grip tightening on the collar of his pathetic shirt, yanking him toward me. I hiss, every word dripping venom, "Two fucking million down the drain, and you think a store and some 'other things' from your pretty fake wife will settle it?"

"Believe me, she is..." David's lips tug upward in a sly smile, revealing a darkness he thinks he's hiding, "a beauty."

*Motherfucking creep.*

It would be so easy to just off this two-bit conman. *Sure.*

*But killing him?*

That's just inviting unnecessary heat, and I've got enough of that already. Besides, Rivington Street's got enough dead bodies without us adding to the tally. The fucking police have their panties in a bunch trying to pin us on some cartel shootouts...on Rivington Street, of all places. Everyone knows that's junkie central, not our playground.

I laugh.

Fucking hell, the idea that we'd deal in flesh. As if I'd stoop so low. But let's get one thing straight: I might run a tight ship, but the whole flesh market? Nah, that's not our style.

*What am I?* The heir to the Morozov Bratva.

Not some lowlife from Brighton Beach.

I don't need to stoop to the basest levels of criminality. I have standards, *derr'mo*.

The next second, Mikhail's hand collides with David's face, a smack so ferocious that blood fills David's mouth instantly. I can almost hear the tear of flesh, his cheek brutally grating against the sharp edges of his teeth.

*Misha is really enjoying this.*

David's wriggling around like a damned fish out of water, blood dripping from the corner of his mouth, ropes cutting into his wrists. Misha, that beast, just stands there wiping David's blood from his knuckles onto his pants as if he's brushing off some dirt.

Sure, I've got the height, but Misha? He's built like a fucking tank. Those scars, the scruffy beard, they've seen more shit than the sewers of this city. But it's those hawk-like eyes, piercing and calculating, that make men piss their pants. Right now, they're drilling into David, and not in a kind way.

"Thought you'd just waltz outta this one with that stupid smirk, huh?" Misha says, every word dripping with an amusement that could freeze hell.

David's reduced to a sniveling mess, the cocky bastard from earlier gone, replaced by this… puddle.

"You fucked up big time, David," I chime in, my grin wide, enjoying every damn second. "Where's the girl?" I ask.

David's choking back sobs, spitting out words between gasps. "She's… She's at Thompson Tales. Fifth Ave."

*Fuck, I love money, always have.*

And if I can squeeze out every last dime from that bookstore and have a bit of fun with the woman running it?

*I wonder if Laura will break as easily.*

"What… what are you going to do with her?" David barely gets the words out, his voice more air than sound.

Misha just eyes David with a look that promises pain. "We'll do whatever the fuck we want, David. Playtime's just beginning." He stands, straightening his suit like he's preparing for a business meeting. "Stay the fuck in town." Without another word, he's out the door.

David, still on the floor, his voice strained, mutters, "You're all fucking monsters. Laura doesn't deserve this shit."

*This bastard's more fucked in the head than I thought. Who offers up their "wife" to bail out of their fuck-ups, then acts like he fucking cares?*

I'm inches away from slamming my boot into his face. Holding back, I lean down, my voice a deadly whisper as I say, "When you dance with demons, David, expect to get burned."

That girl's in for a world of hurt, and she doesn't even know it.

# Chapter 2

*Laura*

**THE BUZZ** of my phone drags me out of the light sleep I had managed to catch at my desk. A slew of unpaid bills for the store lie scattered around, with numbers that seem to have way too many zeros. Ah, a reminder of another sleepless night trying to figure out how the hell to dig myself out of this financial pit after David, my husband of three years, cleaned out our bank account before disappearing with Polly two months ago.

How does one man manage to be cliche and original at the same time?

Most men have affairs, but not all of them drain your bank account and disappear into the wind with the side chick. As for Polly, I hope she likes her men unreliable and with the personality depth of a puddle.

Groaning, I pick up the phone. An unknown number. Great, probably another creditor or, better yet, a robocall telling me I've won a free cruise. Because, you know, three in the morning is prime telemarketing time, right?

"Who's this?" I answer, voice groggy.

"Ms. Thompson?"

"Yeah, still me. And if you're trying to sell me something, I'd prefer bankruptcy advice right now," I retort, one eye on those damned bills.

There's an unsettling pause.

Suddenly, a chill prickles up my neck. *Wait, did they find David? Dead in a ditch somewhere?*

*Or… is that just wishful thinking? God…I'm probably reserving a spot in hell.*

"This is the fire department."

My heart does a weird lurch thing in my chest. A bad sign.

*Okay. It's not about David.*

*But fuck, why are you calling me at unholy o'clock?*

"We're at Thompson Tales of Fifth Ave. There's a fire."

I can't even muster a sarcastic comeback. That's new. "My store?" My voice comes out in a hoarse whisper, which is embarrassing. I clear my throat. "Is it… bad?"

"I think you need to see for yourself."

I frantically search for something—anything—to wear that isn't doused in yesterday's melancholy. I grab the first thing I feel: an old, faded nighty with a cheesy *"Seduce me with paragraphs, tease me with prose"* print. Damn, I thought I'd thrown this monstrosity out. My fingers snag on a lightweight cardigan, which I drape over myself as an afterthought, more for coverage than warmth. It's November in New

York, after all, and the last thing I need is frostbite in places best left unmentioned.

Living a few blocks away from my store had always been a point of pride. No commute, no morning rush, and the extra savings? That was the cherry on top.

A chilly wind picks up, tossing my hair wildly and making me second-guess the wisdom of those mismatched flip-flops I'd thrown on. Each step feels like an eternity, the chilled air biting at my toes and seeping up the hem of my nighty.

I hustle down the streets, the wind funneling through the urban canyons, forcing me to squint against its force. Every breath is a sharp sting, and I start coughing from the cold air slashing down my throat.

Damnit. It's like inhaling ice shards.

There's a low, gravelly laugh up ahead. A guy, definitely drunk and feeling a little too cocky, lurches from a darkened doorway. "Hey there, Cinderella, looking for your prince?" he slurs, leering at me.

"Only if he's carrying a fire extinguisher," I snap back, pushing past him.

As I get closer, there's a distinct smell that hits me. The scent of scorched paper, burned wood, and a lingering, acrid stench that makes my eyes water.

And, well, shit.

My bookstore is charred. Like "There's not gonna be a sequel" kind of charred.

All those hours, days, years… up in literal smoke.

*Fuck.*

*Fuck. Shit. Fuck.*

*This is not happening!*

Flames. Everywhere. Thompson Tales of Fifth Ave is an inferno at three a.m. Even the moon hides behind clouds, not wanting to witness the demise of my bookstore. My family's legacy.

I stand, alone and cold, on the opposite street, with just the firefighters for company. They're busy, their frantic movements dancing with the cruel, golden flickers that consume every memory of my store.

A firefighter is desperately aiming water at what's left of my storefront.

*Oh, my God.*

That holiday window display I'd spent hours on last week? Annihilated. Dad had said it was a wasted effort, but the recent uptick in foot traffic begged to differ. My plans for the Christmas book readings, the New Year's author meet-and-greet, and even that little corner I'd set aside for kids to dive into their first novels… all up in smoke now. Literal smoke.

*Oh God, no.*

The wail of sirens grows louder as I near the scene like some morbid alarm clock reminding me this isn't a nightmare. The gleam of fire trucks pierces through the foggy haze, workers in uniform scrambling everywhere, directing powerful streams at the skeletal remains of what was my everything. Suddenly, a firm hand stops me, an officer's stern face appearing through the smog.

"You can't get closer, ma'am."

I squint at him. "You think?"

He doesn't seem to appreciate my sarcasm. "Safety protocols."

"Just wanted a front-row seat to my life going up in smoke," I quip, even though my heart's breaking with every water-soaked page that flies by.

The words spill out before I can stop them. His eyes widen briefly before he composes himself.

My eyes sting, not from the smoke, but from the emotions threatening to spill over. "I'm so sorry," I force out, fighting the urge to break down. I've always believed public meltdowns are reserved for dramatic movie scenes and not real life.

Gathering some semblance of dignity, I continue, "I own that... well, what was once a store."

His eyes mellow for a moment. "Look, I get it. This is awful, and I'm truly sorry," he says, genuine sympathy evident in his voice. "We only got the call an hour ago. The flames had already taken hold by the time we arrived."

I nearly snort, but it comes out more like a choked sob. "An hour ago?"

He exhales, obviously trying to maintain patience. "We respond as soon as we're alerted. It's never fast enough in situations like these."

My hands fly to my mouth, pressing against my lips as I attempt to keep the sob trapped inside. The weight of the moment presses down, threatening to crush me.

His posture softens. "I wish there was more we could've done."

Trembling, I fish out my phone from the depths of my bag, almost instinctively wanting to dial David's number. It's a force of habit, the kind of thing you do when you've been with someone for as long as we were. My thumb hovers over his name. It's then I remember the ridiculous Post-it note.

*Sorry, Laura.*

*Sorry? You're sorry?!*

*You run off with Polly Pocket, empty our bank account, and all I get is a Post-it?!*

I imagine that square yellow piece of paper—one stuck so haphazardly near our shoe rack that it took me hours to find it amidst the chaos he left behind. *Oh*, and the delightful realization that followed: the emptied bank account, the missing savings—ninety-nine point nine percent of it earned by my own sweat.

Him and my twenty-year-old assistant Polly, enjoying each other's company behind my unsuspecting back for months. Little Polly, whom I had almost mothered, who couldn't tell a P&L statement from a grocery list, had betrayed me, too, helping herself to the cash in the bookstore before fleeing with my husband.

*How the hell did I miss that?*

Recalling it makes my blood boil. David's face on our wedding day, promising forever. Then, those recent distant eyes. Maybe they weren't lies. Maybe they were just preludes to that damned Post-it note.

Like a fresh slap, reminding me of all the times I've been called "naïve" and "clueless," especially by my dad. Dad would have a field day with this.

"This is what you get, Laura," I can almost hear him sneer. "Always trusting everyone, thinking the world's some bloody fairytale. You never listened, never learned." He'd always been quick to point out my missteps, every stumble, every blunder. "Your lack of foresight is astounding, Laura." When David vanished with our life savings, Dad had only one thing to say: "Typical. Trusting a snake and then acting shocked when it bites? That's on you." The accusatory tone, the condescending smirk… it's always the same.

The pain of betrayal by David was one thing, but having to report it to the police was its own circle of hell. The embarrassment of sitting there, recounting my naivety, watching as the officer's eyes didn't even flicker with surprise.

"Another case of a runaway spouse," he'd muttered, scribbling down notes, making me feel like just another statistic, another foolish wife left in the lurch. But what stung most? The officer's indifference mirrored how Dad would've reacted.

Just another day, another *Laura mess-up*.

With a sigh, I contemplate the train wreck my life's become, then decide a chat with Serena might just be what the doctor ordered. I scroll to her name in my contacts, a smile tugging at the corner of my lips despite the chaos.

There it is: **"Gothic Goddess Ser."** My bestie, emotional anchor, and Paranormal Romance Scribe Extraordinaire.

Ser always knows how to weave a bit of magic into the darkest tales, both in her writing and in real life.

Just seeing her caller ID makes me tear up more.

I instantly realize there are two missed calls and a graveyard of unread texts from her, mostly filled with her raving about some vampire and witch love triangle she's cooking up. Ever since college, she's been engrossed in her otherworldly tales. I reminisce about those late-night brainstorming sessions, with me pitching dark, steamy romance scenes and her laughing, her curly hair bouncing as she typed away. James, her partner-in-crime since our uni days, would be somewhere in the background, lost in his political spy drama.

But right now, she doesn't pick up.

I guess I'll drop her a message then. Typing is... harder than expected. My fingers hover for a moment, and then I begin, each word a weight off my chest:

*"Hey, Ser... Store's gone. Burned toast style. Could use... idk, that thing where we eat too much ice cream, cry over trashy romcoms, and fart without judgment. Please."*

After I hit "send," unease hits me.

It's not just the fire anymore.

There's a small crowd forming. It's almost 5.30 a.m. Then, out of the corner of my eye, a figure stands apart from the crowd. A tall, imposing figure stands in the distance. The fog and smoke curl around him, shrouding him in an aura of menace. His head turns, seemingly scanning the onlookers, and my stomach plummets. For a split second, our gazes lock. That look. It's cold, calculating—like a predator spotting a wounded prey.

His eyes narrow, giving away nothing, yet everything.

And just as quickly as the chill from his gaze seeps into me, he turns and fades into the dark alley.

Just like that, he's gone.

# Chapter 3

*Laura*

**YAAAWN...**

I drag my hands over my weary eyes as a massive yawn takes over.

Sunlight bleeds through the haze, revealing the blackened ruins of what was once Thompson Tales of Fifth Ave. Exhaustion tugs at my eyes, and every muscle in my body aches with a weariness that's more than just physical.

God, I look like a dumpster fire—fitting, given the circumstances.

I squint against the blinding glare, taking in the twisted metal, the scorched wood, and the smell. That pungent, burned smell. "That was my future," I mutter, as if saying it out loud makes any difference.

A firefighter, still finishing up, glances my way, then quickly looks away.

Pity?

Yeah, no need. I've got a full stock of that in my inventory.

I reach for my coffee, cold and bitter, much like my life at this moment.

Suddenly, the cup slips, splashing its contents over my shirt.

"Great, just great!" I snap, the liquid's cold sting a perfect metaphor for my luck. I toss the empty cup aside, rubbing at the stain as if I could erase this mishap along with my string of bad luck.

"Of course," I grimace. Damnit, this sums up the day. "Why not add coffee stains to the mix?"

Deciding a closer look at the smoldering aftermath of my "future" is necessary, I head toward the entrance. Spotting a firefighter conferring with his team, I take a deep breath and interrupt. "Can I go in?" My voice cracks, nausea rising in my throat.

He turns to me, eyes sizing up the clear desperation on my face. After what feels like an eternity, he says, "You the owner?"

I nod, swallowing hard.

Pushing through the haze and fatigue, I wait for his response. This guy, looking all rugged intensity, seems like he's straight out of an action movie poster—hardened by fire, eyes a shade too penetrating.

He gives me the once-over, eyes lingering a tad too long on the unfortunate coffee stain splashed across my shirt's audacious print: "Seduce me with paragraphs, tease me with prose." Oh, and let's not forget the fashion debacle down south—mismatched flip-flops.

Stellar.

His gruff response breaks through my internal cringe-fest.

"You can head in with me," he rumbles, "but hands off. Still figuring out this mess."

The moment I step over the threshold, the atmosphere changes. Sounds echo oddly—water drips, beams groan in protest, and there's the distant hum of police radios. Shadows play tricks, making the destroyed sections of the shop morph into grotesque shapes.

Tip-toeing through, I reach what was once a vibrant romance aisle. Those stories, filled with heated glances and stolen kisses, now burned to ashes. From a distance, someone yells, "Clear on this side!" and I see a firefighter passing by, giving me a nod. I take it as an all-clear sign.

"You know," I turn to the rugged action-hero lookalike, "I didn't envision my day starting like this." I'm holding in tears that are about to roll down my cheeks.

He nods, an understanding look in his eyes. "We're doing our best to handle the situation. But I must say, considering the circumstances, you're handling this remarkably well."

I let out a sardonic laugh. "What can I say? Guess I'm just trying to keep it together."

He glances around the charred remnants of the shop. "It's tough, especially when it's something close to your heart. We see it often, but it doesn't get easier."

Sighing, I admit, "It's more than just a shop. It's memories, history… my life?"

There's an unexpected gentleness in his eyes now. "For what it's worth, I'm sorry."

Before I can respond, a voice crackles on his radio, pulling his attention. "Got it," he responds, giving me a last measured look before heading back to his crew. I'm left amidst the ruins.

Glancing at what's left of a wall, memories flash. There once stood wooden shelves and that unmistakably vintage table. Oh, that table.

Grandpa's proud purchase from a Brooklyn flea market back when opening this shop was just a wild idea. Seems like "vintage" wasn't fireproof. Who knew?

It was also Mrs. Anderson's favorite corner, where the latest mystery book and a steaming cup of tea were her trusty companions. She'd sink into the stories, living them as vividly as her tea steeped next to her.

Now, the firefighters are the main characters in this tragic play, moving around what remains of my family's legacy. I squint around; yeah, it's not looking promising. There's a chatter of officers, sounds of radios, and the footsteps of firefighters doing… firefighter things, I guess.

I laugh.

Not because it's funny, but because it's that or cry. This place, bursting with stories and dreams, has turned into a place where officers now gather clues instead of kids gathering for story hour.

And the smell, God, the smell.

Burned pages and wet wood, a parody of the old and comforting aroma of well-loved books and ancient dust that used to welcome me every day.

It's just wrong, all of it.

I feel like I am caught in a bad joke where everything dear to me is the punchline. It's tragic, sarcastic, and oh-so-New-York all at once.

I hold my breath.

The harsh remnants below me press into my skin, reminding me sharply, painfully, ironically, of every lost possibility that once lived here. It's not just a building that's in ruins; it's memories, it's legacies, it's my damned life.

This moment, right after a catastrophe, everything is too loud yet eerily silent, settles around me. The wailing sirens, the bystanders murmuring—it all becomes a muffled backdrop to the chaotic symphony playing in my head.

Thoughts like, *"Why didn't I upgrade the fire system?"*

Thoughts like, *"This store was my family's legacy."*

Thoughts like, *"How do I break it to Dad without ending up in the family doghouse?"*

Thoughts like, *"I need a drink so strong it could perhaps put me to sleep for a million years."*

A crunch of debris under boots snatches me from my brewing storm of thoughts.

Footsteps.

I turn, half-expecting it to be him, but it's the firefighter instead, bearing the weary look of one who's seen too much yet has to keep on.

Snap out of it, Laura. It's been two months. The man's gone, and wishing won't drag him through that door.

"Ms...?" He trails off, checking his clipboard.

"Thompson. Laura Anne Thompson," I fill in, and his eyes flit over the ruins, making a silent tally of despair.

"Ms. Thompson, we suspect the fire started from the pantry area," he continues, glancing toward the dark, ash-coated room where I used to sneak snacks during the slow hours. "Our preliminary investigation suggests an electrical fault might've triggered it. We found some faulty wiring, quite ancient, running through the place."

So, it wasn't the ghosts of old authors or a grudge-bearing rival bookstore. It was something as mundane as decayed wires deciding to bow out with a spark.

He glances around one more time before locking eyes with me. "We're still investigating, but you might want to contact your insurance company. Provide them with the initial findings; it will expedite the claim process."

His words clang around my head like loose change.

Insurance. Claims. Dad.

My tongue feels heavy in my mouth. "Thank you… Officer…?"

"Bennett. Firefighter Bennett," he replies, with a nod.

I give him a weak smile, grappling for composure. "Thank you, Bennett. I appreciate your efforts."

He seems to sense my internal struggle. "Fires are destructive, Ms. Thompson, but they can also pave the way for new beginnings. Thompson Tales of Fifth Ave might rise from these ashes, stronger."

His words should be a comfort, but all I can think of is the impending call to my father, the dance of disappointment, and the blame game.

"Yeah," I answer, attempting to inject some optimism into my voice, "a phoenix, right? Rises from the ashes and all that."

Bennett smiles, a gesture that doesn't quite reach his eyes, filled with the somber knowledge of things lost and battles fought. "Exactly. Take care, Ms. Thompson. If there's anything else, don't hesitate to reach out."

Damnit, I need some fresh air.

I stumble out of my charred shop, only to spot bystanders with phones out, snapping pictures and shooting videos. Great, just what I need—the paparazzi moment I never asked for. Because apparently, having your life go up in smoke isn't enough; it needs to go viral, too. Talk about hitting rock bottom with an audience.

Great, Laura, now what?

I chew on my nails, a nervous tic I've never managed to shake. Dad's going to find out, and the thought of breaking the news about the store? That's a conversation I'm not looking forward to.

Fuck.

Then, my eyes get caught on something else. A sleek, dark sedan, far too luxurious for this part of town, sits conspicuously across the street... It screams money, looking like it took a wrong turn from Park Avenue and ended up in my less-than-glamorous neighborhood. My store's been here for years, and I've never seen this car model, not once. It's positioned perfectly, like it has a front-row seat to my downfall.

"Enjoying the view?" I quip under my breath, my voice laced with bitterness.

As if on cue, there's a click. Someone's emerging.

But before I can put a face to the mysterious car owner, Serena's voice cuts through the fog. "Lu Lu! Holy hell, are you okay?"

Turning, I find my best friend Serena hurrying toward me, her vibrant curls bouncing with each step. Her face is a mix of concern and shock. "Ser," I croak out, tears threatening to spill, "it's all... just gone."

She wraps me in a hug, a warm protective cocoon against the world's cruelties. "We got you, LuLu. Oh, my God. Thank God you are okay."

Pulling away, I glance back toward the sedan, but all I see is an empty parking spot. The car vanished.

"Was there...?" I start, pointing vaguely to where the sedan had been.

Serena follows my gaze, her brows knitting in confusion. "What are you talking about?"

The pit in my stomach grows. "Nothing, it's just... Never mind."

# Chapter 4

*Victor*

**CLUB V**

The bass thumps in my chest as I stride into the club, my footsteps in sync with the heartbeat of this place. It's mine, after all—every plush seat, every polished glass, every drop of top-shelf liquor. And by the looks of it tonight, every scantily clad woman with a predatory gleam in her eye. The grand chandeliers cast a dim glow, making the gold and marble décor glint.

"Victor!" one calls out, a sultry redhead in a dress that leaves very little to the imagination. She runs a finger along the curve of her collarbone, batting eyelashes thick with mascara.

Ignoring her is as easy as breathing.

Another, a leggy blond with a neckline plunging to the navel, sidles up, offering her most practiced pout. "Victor, a drink?" she purrs, tracing a finger along my forearm.

"No, not today," I retort, brushing her off, my attention already elsewhere.

As I make my way, I can hear the chorus of disappointed sighs and the muttered curses from the rejected. The women in this joint might look like they stepped out of a high-end magazine, but they're vultures, each one of them. The gold-plated counters, the shimmering drapes, and the chandeliers—all flaunting the obscene amounts of cash that flow through Club V every damn night. We're talking a few hundred grand on booze alone, and don't get me started on what these depraved souls spend on their drug fixes.

I might own this place, but I'd be damned if I give these gold-diggers even a whiff of what they want. They're after one thing: a quick ticket to the high life on my dime.

Not happening. *Ever.*

"All good, boss?" A deep voice pulls me from my thoughts. Luka, my club manager, stands beside me. A solid wall of a man in his early 30s, wearing a slick black suit that stretches a bit too tight across his broad shoulders. The glare from his bald head is almost as sharp as the predatory glint in his eyes. But beneath that exterior, the guy's got a head for numbers and runs this place tighter than a drum.

"Everything running smoothly?" I ask, keeping my tone even.

"Like clockwork," Luka rumbles, adjusting his thick gold chain. "VIP section's filled up, and the new shipment's in the back. We're gonna make a fucking killing tonight."

"Language, Luka. We're businessmen, not street thugs." I smirk, taking a sip of my drink.

He snorts. "Says the man who could snap someone in two without breaking a sweat."

I arch an eyebrow, not rising to the bait. "Anything else?"

Luka glances around, ensuring we're not overheard. "Got a tip-off. Feds might be snooping around. Might want to keep the backroom activities low-key tonight."

I nod. "Thanks for the heads up. Just make sure the patrons are happy and our earnings remain sky-high. As for our… other business, we can always resume tomorrow."

The deep beats of the club pulse around me; my gaze narrows, meticulously scanning the crowd. It doesn't take long for me to pick them out. Two men, dressed a bit too sharply, sipping on their overpriced vodka and feigning interest in the women around them. Their eyes, however, are firmly locked on me, tracking my every move. Fucking undercover feds, I'm sure of it. I've been in this game long enough to spot a rat, and these guys reek of it.

"Fucking Vasiliev," I mutter under my breath. The tip-off had to be from him. Only Ivan Vasiliev would be low enough to send the feds my way in the middle of a goddamn Friday night. It's a move straight out of his playbook. Subtle but unmistakable. He might have climbed his way to the top through sheer ruthlessness, but I was born into this life. And while he was busy building his empire, I was learning the trade—every dirty trick, every nuance.

A waiter swings by, offering drinks from a tray. I wave him off and continue to survey my domain. Club V is my fortress, my ground, and nobody, especially not Ivan or his snitches, is going to challenge that.

Grabbing my drink, I make my move. Walking with purpose, I head straight toward the two undercover agents, deciding to play this my way.

"Gentlemen," I greet them, my voice dripping with faux warmth. "Enjoying your night?"

They exchange a glance, clearly not expecting the direct approach. Good. Keep them on their toes.

One of them, a tall, broad-shouldered guy with a bad comb-over, forces a smile. "Just a night out with the boys. Heard this place was the best in town."

"Indeed, it is," I reply with a smirk. "Just remember to play nice. We have a strict policy against unwanted... attention."

The second one, younger, with nervous eyes, clears his throat. "We'll keep that in mind."

With a nod, I leave them be, heading back to the heart of my club.

Let them stew on that.

Let Ivan stew on that, the *suka*.

If they want a war, I'm ready. Always have been.

---

Taking a swig of my drink, I lounge in the VIP area, elevated just enough to look down on all the peasants grinding away on the dance floor. It's quieter up here, shielded from the rabble by my muscle—the security team that guards the entrance.

The layout's clean and minimalistic—black leather couches, dim blue lights, and a private bar with the most expensive shit money can buy. Not that the décor matters; it's all about power. From here, I can scope out everyone. The bottom-feeders, the leeches, the bloodsuckers. The cartel bosses, with their flashy suits and heavy gold chains, thinking they own the place. A few of them shoot impatient glances my way, itching for a chat. But today? *Nahuy*.

Not in the mood.

Let them wait.

The game's all about patience, after all.

A sudden vibration of my phone shatters my peace, an annoying buzz in my pocket. Yanking it out, the screen flashes a message so stark it almost makes me laugh.

**Misha:** *David's gone. Gathering his shit. You'll have it in twenty-four hours.*

I laugh. What a fucking surprise.

And, of course, the damn old bookstore goes up in flames a day after David signs it over.

Typical, the cowardly shit, slinking away from the messes he makes. After stirring up a goddamn hornet's nest, he has the balls to just slip away?

Oh, I'll hunt him down, alright, drag him back by his hair if I have to. He's up to his neck in this, and I swear I'll make him drown in it. Because no one, absolutely no one, fucks with Victor Morozov and walks away breathing.

And as for *Laura*, she's collateral now.

*Blyad.*

Trailing Laura this morning was supposed to be straightforward, but shit, she caught me off guard.

I didn't expect her to be breathtaking.

My mind reels back to this morning: She's running, cheeks red, breath steaming out in the cold like an exhaust pipe. Her auburn hair's a wild cascade, making me itch to yank it back to see those eyes cloud with desire as she moans.

I shadow her, hungry for another glimpse. But damn, she looks more beautiful, with those tear-filled eyes, staring at the ashes of that dump she called a bookstore—pathetically beautiful.

I almost feel bad. *Almost.*

Honestly, I could've paid for ten of those trashy stores with what I make in an hour. I didn't need that bookstore; it was peanuts to the empire I built. But debt? It's a matter of principle. As my old man, the *Pakhan*, would always drill into my head: "Never let a debt go unpaid, especially if it's owed to you."

The very thought of her has my heart pounding uncontrollably, and the unwanted surge of blood has my cock straining against my slacks.

Fucking inconvenient.

I slam back my vodka, hoping to drown the itch to get another look at her.

"*Chert voz'mi,*" I swear under my breath.

Glancing downward, I scan the swarm of bodies in my club. It's just another Friday night, meant for some fun. But hell, no one's stirring any wicked urges in me tonight.

What's wrong with me?

Out of nowhere, a form draws my attention — the radiant hue of auburn locks, a body's curve I'd recognize anywhere.

*No way, is that...?*

It's *her.*

My eyebrows pull together seeing what she's wearing.

*Oh, sweet mother of God.*

*That dress on her?*

Fuck, it's like it's vacuum-sealed onto her, every damn curve popping out and begging for attention. Too tight around her tits and ass, like she's wearing it just to screw with me.

*What the hell is she doing here?*

"Victor," a sultry voice slinks into my ear like oil over water.

Fucking Eleni, always in my VIP area. I swear she's either got dirt on my guys, or she just knows how to play them right.

She never misses a Friday night, despite how fucking livid her father, Costas Theodorou of the notorious Theodorou Greece mafia clan, would be if he found out she's dancing in my club. Tonight, she's decked out in gold, trying her hardest to outshine everything else.

"Missed me?" she purrs. Her cold, entitled hand makes its way to my groin.

*No fucking way.* Fucking her once was all it took to know she was more in love with her own voice than anything else. And by anything, I mean anything.

"I missed you," she drawls, her Greek accent thick and intentional.

I pry her hand off, holding back the urge to snap. "Not now, Eleni. Fuck off."

She pouts, looking all wounded. What a performance. "You're such an ass, Victor."

I smirk. "You knew that when you climbed into bed with me."

But she's already become background noise because my attention's riveted on *her*—the unexpected guest in the tight red dress and her many shots of whiskey.

*Laura.*

A thrill surges within me.

# Chapter 5

*Laura*

"ONE MORE, please!"

I try to outshout the pulsating bass as I gesture for another whiskey shot to a bartender. She nods and promptly pours the golden liquid into the glass before placing it in front of me.

Swallowing the shot in one go, the burn of the whiskey contrasts sharply with the cold pinch of the dress. As I set the empty glass on the counter, I lock eyes with the too-cool-for-school bartender and gesture for one more.

*What the hell was I thinking?*

After witnessing my bookstore reduced to ashes today, I should be at home, spoon-deep in Ben & Jerry's, drowning in tears and comfy blankets.

But here I am. Can't sit thanks to this dress that's two sizes too small. Can't stand because, with every bass thud, I feel another part of me jiggle. Honestly, Ben & Jerry's was the smarter choice. The frigid air of Club V isn't doing me any favors, either, making my nipples prickle from the chill and reminding me exactly how exposed my ass cheeks feel in this getup.

*Damnit, Serena, where the hell are you?*

How in the world did she even talk me into this? *Right.* The promise of an exclusive VIP entrance and endless free whiskey. "It's a promotional thing for my book business," she'd said, batting her eyelashes innocently. "Come on, it'll be fun!"

*Fun.* Right. And now she's nowhere to be found.

"Why'd you even come?" I muse aloud, though I'm not sure if I'm asking myself or the silent bartender.

I fish out my phone from my purse, the screen illuminating a string of missed calls and texts.

**Gothic Goddess Ser:** *Hey babe, I am SOOOOO SORRY! Lucas has a fever, and I can't make it to Club V. But try to have fun without me! And find a handsome man to flirt with ;) xoxo. Love yah.*

*Fuck.*

*Fuck shit.*

I shoot back a quick reply.

**Me:** *I want to hate you so much right now. But I can't since it's Lucas… Going home to Ben & Jerry's now.*

Another shot is placed in front of me. Without hesitation, I knock it back. The warmth spreads, and for a moment, the room starts to spin just a little.

"Damnit, Ser," I mutter, more to myself than anyone else. The alcohol quickly courses through me, blurring my usually razor-sharp judgment.

"Sounds like someone stood you up." The voice is a creepy, too-friendly lilt and far too close. I turn my head slowly, already regretting my decision to come tonight. Before me stands a man, his hair clinging to his scalp in a losing battle against baldness, the fluorescent lights from the bar accentuating each glistening sweat bead on his forehead. His shirt is stretched over an ample belly, the top few buttons threatening to pop off.

"More like abandoned for a toddler with a fever. But who's keeping track?" I shout back, my throat straining to be heard over the pounding music, the effort scratching at my throat, making me wince.

*Don't be friendly, Laur.*

*Don't start a conversation. Go home.*

His beady eyes, which have been roaming all over my body, finally settle on my face, but not for long. "Well, lucky me, then." His grin reveals yellowed teeth and a sickly-sweet odor wafts from him, reminding me of rotten fruit mixed with stale beer.

"Yeah, quite the unexpected evening," I retort, my voice a bit sharper than I'd like. I attempt to steady myself, but the alcohol's grip makes it difficult. The floor feels unsteady, or maybe it's just my legs.

I can't decide.

His eyes are now on my tits, and his fingers twitch as if they have a mind of their own. I can almost feel their clammy touch on my skin without him actually touching me.

"You look like you need some… company," he slurs, swaying a little too close to my personal space.

"I'm good, thanks," I retort, trying to edge away, but he steps in closer, his greasy presence now almost suffocating.

"You sure about that, doll?" He leers, the look in his eyes growing darker.

I take a deep breath, reminding myself that scenes in public places are best avoided. "Absolutely. In fact, I was just leaving."

"Already? The night's just getting started." He snickers. "Or you can leave with me…"

His hand slaps down, clammy and presuming, claiming territory on my waist like he's planting a flag. A thumb grazes my breast, a move so bold it could be in neon lights. My skin crawls. My temper flares.

*Crap. Crap on a cracker.*

"Perhaps another time." I picture myself as slicing through his sleazy little fantasy. My fingers curl around his wrist, and I use all my might to peel his grip off me, like stripping tape from a new package.

"Who you waiting for?" he slurs, his words sloppy as he clumsily reaches for my wrist again.

*I'm really not in the mood for this.*

"My boyfriend," I stammer, aiming for vague.

"Yeah, right," he snorts, barely standing straight.

I arch an eyebrow, my patience wearing thin. "And you'd know because…?"

*Shut it, Laura. Don't engage.*

"Seen 'em all… Y'all comin' in, hopin' for that… whatchamacallit? Special someone? And then, boom! Nothin'." His voice slurs, like he's in on some club joke I'm missing.

I have a strong urge to escape. "Well, if you'll excuse me," I begin, trying to sidestep him. "I need to find my boyfriend now."

He's swaying like a skyscraper in a high wind, blocking me with that lumbering body of his. "Don't kid yourself, pretty doll," he slurs, his breath a distillery's nightmare. "You're just trolling for deep pockets…" And bam, his clammy hand slaps onto my butt.

"Hey!" I snap, my voice sharp, twisting away from him. I slap his hand, but he grabs onto me even harder. I push his hands off as hard as I can. "What the hell do you think you're doing?"

"Aw, jus' havin' some fun, doll," he slurs through his clumsy lips, that greasy smirk unfaltering.

"Yeah, by grabbing me?" I snap back in anger.

He shrugs nonchalantly, the alcohol making his movements exaggerated. "Was just tryin' to appreciate ya," he mumbles, his words nearly blending together. "Don't see why you gotta be so uptight 'bout it."

"Get your fucking hands off me!" I struggle.

He gets closer, his foul breath mixing with the ambient scent of spilled drinks and sweaty bodies. "Don't act so stuck-up, doll. I saw you alone, figured you'd be grateful for the attention."

I can feel my heart kicking against my ribs.

*Seriously, anybody… please*

As if on cue, the music cuts, and the club plunges into an unexpected quiet.

I tug fiercely, trying to escape the constricting grip on my arm. Then, a voice cold with promise pierces the stillness, "Get your fucking hands off my woman."

I'm looking all over the dim club, trying to figure out who's talking. There's this exciting but kinda risky vibe in the air. Then, like the sun finally breaking through the clouds, he comes out from some shadowy spot. Like a dark knight.

Could've sworn he just walked out of those spicy romance books I can't put down. He's the living, breathing version of the dark ink and grumpy mystery guys who fill those pages.

My mouth's bone-dry, and my armpits are working overtime. My body's shouting a full-blown, caps-locked *WOW*.

My eyes involuntarily rake over him, lingering on places I've no business staring at. It's like my pupils have turned into little heat-seeking missiles, targeting all the hot spots. My cheeks flare up, the heat undeniable.

I've never ogled someone this shamelessly. The thought hits me—maybe clothes are just doing him a disservice. I blink, surprised at my dirty thoughts.

*Where did that come from?*

His eyes, so intense and penetrating, seem to recognize something in me, or maybe it's the other way around.

A memory niggles at the back of my mind. Wait, have I seen him before? Those eyes, that stance, the way he's looking at me now… It's like déjà vu, a scene from a past I can't quite recall.

*Gosh, that whiskey's kicking in strong now.*

Mr. Grabby Hands, still audaciously maintaining his grip on my ass, seems to shrink with every advancing step of my defender. He manages to squeak out a feeble, "F-fuck off!"

With a voice that sounds like it's used to giving orders and having them followed, Mr. Tall, Dark, and Lethal warns, "Back off before I make sure those dirty hands can't touch another damn thing. Especially not my woman."

Hold up. *His what now?*

I must've been dreaming.

Or drunk.

Or both.

With a swiftness that surprises me, he snatches me away from Mr. Grabby Hands and pulls me right into his personal bubble of designer cologne and testosterone. Our faces are so close that I can almost see my shocked reflection in his eyes.

*What is going on here?*

Holy hell, is it even legal to be this tall? That scent of his—it's downright sinful.

His grip on my waist tightens, pure strength radiating from his hand. It's like getting hit with a jolt—like someone's plugged me straight into an electric socket, and all the charge is heading straight to my core. Who knew a mere touch could make a girl feel this… orgasmic?

I mean, seriously?

I look up at him, eyes wide. That intoxicating masculine energy envelops me. He pulls me closer, and my head hits his hard chest.

*Holy hell.*

I'm about one deep breath away from making a scene that would make a romance novel look G-rated.

Suddenly, from the corner of my eye, I catch a few of Mr. Grabby Hands' cronies shifting, their intentions clear. They're gearing up for a brawl, probably hoping to even the odds. Bad idea. Before they can make their move, a pack of sturdy men in crisp black suits, who apparently accompany my mysterious defender, step in, forming a barrier between us and the incoming threat.

Who are these guys? Ninja bouncers?

But what takes the cake is the main event: Mr. Grabby Hands, perhaps fueled by liquid courage or sheer stupidity, makes a move toward the man, clearly underestimating the situation. Bad move. In a swift motion, my defender sidesteps, grabs his arm, and twists it behind his back, pushing him down to his knees.

"Consider this a warning, Roberto," he hisses into Mr. Grabby Hands' ear while maintaining a vise-like grip. Roberto, now clearly regretting his life choices, nods fervently, hoping to escape this night with all limbs intact.

Releasing him, my defender stands tall, watching as Roberto and his posse stumble away, clearly outmatched and outclassed.

Turning those fierce eyes to me, he asks, "You okay?" His voice is a blend of concern and restrained power, making my heart race.

*Breathe, Laura, breathe.*

His gray eyes delve, holding me captive in an unbreakable stare.

"I…"

*Oh, dear lord.*

My pussy stirs from her eight-month hibernation and urgently signals that despite this man radiating strong *"commitment-phobe with dominance tendencies"* vibes, she's absolutely up for a wild ride.

*Stop it. Damnit.*

Swallowing the lump in my throat, I manage a shaky, "Yeah, thanks to you. But you really didn't need to put on a show just for my benefit…" My voice accidentally ramps up a notch. "And that whole 'my woman' thing…" Suddenly, my volume drops, heat creeping up my face.

His eyes darken, boring into mine.

"Who says it was an act?"

I blink.

*Excuse me?*

Before I can question more, his gaze does a quick sweep over me. "Bad choice, wearing that here."

*What the hell?*

Rude. "Last I checked, my wardrobe wasn't up for discussion," I retort, my chin rising a notch.

His left cheek twitches into a half-smirk, and I realize his hand is still glued to my waist.

He then glances at my too-tight top, a smug look on his face. "You're gonna need clothes that can handle the… overflow," he says, eyeing my tits.

Give me a break.

Enough's enough.

I glide past him, leaving his self-assured bubble.

"Until we *don't* meet again," I quip without looking back.

# Chapter 6

*Laura*

**I'M REELING,** backpedaling on heels that seem to have a vendetta against my balance. The corridor offers a getaway, its **EXIT** sign winking at me like an accomplice in a heist.

*Great, just great.*

Standing as tall as my wobbling stance allows, I pull in my stomach, cursing the too-tight dress that's now an enemy of my breathing.

Maybe Mr. Tall, Dark, Stormy-eyes, and Rude had a point.

*Bad choice, Laura.*

But then again, when have I ever made the right ones?

I risk a glance back at him; there's no mistaking it. Mr. Stormy Eyes is still devouring me with that gaze like I'm his last supper or something.

*Wrong move, Laura.*

His eyes spark with a kind of wild thrill that nearly has me doing the unthinkable—turning my G-string into a water park.

I would like to breathe in his gorgeous roguish five o'clock shadow and dazzlingly white teeth a bit more, but I'd just end up boosting his already big head.

"Stay with me, *Kiska*." he commands.

*Oh. God.*

I clench my pussy tight.

*Come on, feet, don't fail me. March on, and don't you dare stop.*

But I do not march on.

The raw power behind those three words leaves me momentarily dazed. Has anyone ever commanded my attention—my body—with such implicit force?

"Wh-why?" I barely recognize the whisper as my own, my nipples tightening painfully against my dress.

*Damnit, Laura, tear your eyes off him.*

But his gaze intensifies, his gray eyes turning dark, narrowing just slightly, and his tongue darts out to wet his lips. A rush of warmth floods my cheeks.

His eyes lock on mine, nailing me to the spot.

"Let's just say you owe me…" He stops. "Stay for a drink with me. Or are you hurrying back to your… *husband*?"

"I… I don't have a husband. I mean, I *had a* husband, but… but now he is gone," I blurt out.

*Great, Laura, just air your dirty laundry to Mr. High-and-Mighty with a stormy gaze.*

Technically, I've got a husband, but he took off—ran off with Polly and my cash. So, yeah, married, but… *not really.*

Before I can answer myself, Mr. Stormy Eyes sidles up close, and his cologne just about knocks me sideways.

His stare is locked in, like he's trying to crack a safe that is my brain.

With a casual flick of his fingers, he summons over a waitress who scrambles to hand him a glass filled with something that looks suspiciously like it could strip paint.

He offers it to me. "Drink."

I balk. "No. I don't even know your name," I say, trying to sound uninterested, though curiosity is nibbling at me.

He leans in, his lips brushing my ear as he shouts over the pulsing beat. "Victor," he says, and something in his accent makes it sound like he's not just saying his name but casting a spell—Vik-torr.

My G-string is so wet it feels like a flood between my legs. Heat radiates from my core, and I can feel his gaze on my skin.

*Ohmygod.*

*Ohmyfuckinggod.*

*What is he doing to me?*

I pretend to stifle a laugh. "What was that? *Vodka*?" I shout back because it sounds like he's straight out of a Russian spy novel.

I want to run my hands all over him, feel the heat radiating from his body.

*Stop it. Laura.*

*Go home. Laura.*

"Stay, *Laura*," he purrs. He looks like he's used to getting his way, muscles bulging like he bench-presses boulders for fun, clearing the room with just a stare.

For a split second, my brain stops working.

"Wait, how do you even know my name?" My insides are in tumult, and there's a strong urge to just surrender.

"I know everything, *Laura*," he retorts, a dark promise in his voice.

Summoning all the sass I can muster, I fire back, "Including about the pathetic husband who ditched me for my so-called friend and took all my savings?" I confess before I can catch myself.

*Why are you acting like this?*

I don't know why I'm telling him this. Maybe I'm just tired of holding it all in.

He remains unfazed. Those intense eyes never waver, making me want to squirm.

"Guess what? I don't care who you are and what you know. I am leaving." Without another word, I make my exit.

*It's a shame this is the last time I'll see Mr. Cocky Alpha.*

Stumbling slightly, I beeline for the elevator, cursing that, in my quick exit, I left my sweater behind. The street's chill lashes at me, a sobering slap after the club's heat. Desperate, I wave for a cab with numbing fingers.

Luck isn't on my side tonight. It never is. They just rush past me like I'm invisible.

My vision's a blurry mess, each streetlight stretching into streaks. Since 3 a.m., my world's been burning down, literally, and now my body's joining my mind in the rebellion.

Another cab comes into sight. I urge the approaching lights, "C'mon, give a break to a girl who's down on her luck."

I make a wild dash for it, arms flailing like I'm signaling a plane. My heart jumps as the cab slows down, the squeal of brakes sounding like hallelujah. "About time," I say to myself.

*But who am I kidding?*

As if sensing that my life's a mess, it guns the engine and takes off, leaving me in a cloud of dust.

"Seriously?!" My frustration boils over. "Fuck. You!" My voice echoes down the street.

Then, out of nowhere, warmth drapes over me—a coat, heavy and scented with that unmistakable musk… his musk.

# Chapter 7

*Laura*

**I SPIN** on my heel.

*Oh, sweet Jesus.*

There he stands, silhouetted against the streetlights, looking less like a man and more like some sort of nocturnal deity that's stepped right out of myth and into the harsh glow of reality. His gray suit seems to absorb the city's pulse, and his shirt—impossibly white under the moon's gaze—makes him appear all the more unreal.

Men like him don't pursue; they sit on thrones and have the world delivered.

*Unless*, of course, he's got a screw loose and figures I'm today's special on the psycho menu.

"Great," I mutter under my breath. "Stalker much?"

The corner of his mouth twitches. "You look like you could use some help."

I shove his damn coat against that rock-hard armor he calls a chest. "I don't need your help."

*Jesus, what are you packing under there, steel plates?*

The coat hangs between us like a flag of surrender. I'm too pissed to wave properly. He doesn't budge, just cocks an eyebrow, a smirk playing on his lips, as if he's daring me to push harder against the wall of muscle he's masquerading as a man.

My hand's still on his chest, feeling the drumbeat of his heart, a rhythm that seems too steady to be human.

"Would you just take the stupid thing?" My voice comes out half growl, half plea, and I hate the way it cracks.

I stare at him.

He stares back.

A jolt of heat inexplicably sears through me.

*Stop it, Laura. He's a stranger, not your next bad decision.*

The night air sinks its teeth into me. A shiver racks through me, fierce and sharp, and I regret tossing the coat away like I've just chucked my only lifeline back into the sea.

*Fuck.*

Teeth gritted, I let it out blunt and cold: "I don't need your help."

His eyes drop to my dress, and a knowing look crosses his face. "Your dress disagrees."

A blast of cold slaps my cheeks, and *not* the ones on my face. I reach back, and yep, my dress has betrayed me. Bloody hell, there it is; a rip right up to my ass, exposing my freezing cheeks and G-string.

"Give me a break," I snap, flinging the coat back at him with a huff. My hands scramble to cover my backside from his view. Victor's laughter rolls out, deep and smooth, not the reaction I want. It's annoying how it doesn't grind my gears the way it should; how, instead, it sends an odd shiver through me that's not just from the cold.

"You're enjoying this way too much," I grumble, narrowing my eyes at him.

"Interesting," he says, still chuckling.

My eyes do a full orbit in their sockets.

"Care to share what's so fascinating?" I snap, one hand clutching at my skirt in a vain attempt to cover up. "Or is my backside just that entertaining to you?"

Suddenly, his smirk softens into something warm, and it throws me. Didn't peg him for the tender-hearted type.

*Get a grip, Laura!*

"You," he says, "you're quite the firecracker, aren't you?"

It sounds like a compliment, but from him, it feels like he's just sizing me up for his next chess move.

Victor steps in close, too close, but I don't back away.

My brain's yelling *"stranger danger,"* but my body's got its own ideas, leaning toward his warmth. As he covers me with his coat, I flinch, not from cold but from the sudden closeness. Surprisingly, I don't mind the proximity.

My mind's racing, a hamster wheel of *"oh-no-he-didn'ts"* and *"oh-yes-he-dids."*

"Come on," he says, voice all velvet and smoke. "Let me drive you home," he offers. It's oddly tender for a guy who looks like he could snap a neck without breaking a sweat.

*He's offering to take me home?*

There's a twinge in my chest.

Disappointment?

*Seriously?*

What was I hoping for? What? Did I want him to sweep me off to some grand adventure instead?

Those big hands of his are careful as they brush away a curl from my cheek, and I'm suddenly a statue, only I'm feeling everything.

He tugs the coat tighter, and I'm wrapped up in a cloud of his scent. It's like walking into a wall of man—pure, undiluted Victor. It's nothing I've known before, not with David, not with anyone. Suddenly, he's not just a guy; he's *the* guy, and every breath I take is laced with him.

He's not just handsome now; he's something out of a freaking romance novel. And then there's his face inches from mine, lips promising all sorts of sin. His breath doesn't reek. Not like David's always did, that made my stomach flip—in a bad way.

*Stay back*, my brain warns. But who's listening?

I'm done being the good girl who gets walked all over.

I squeeze my legs together, a pathetic defense. It's been too damn long since… well, anything.

I look up and our eyes meet, and there's this dance in his stormy gaze, a flicker that suggests he's seeing more than I'm showing. His pupils dilate, and that damn tongue flicks across his lip. My brain's screaming at me, but my body's been lonely way too long.

*I want him.*

*Fuck. I want him.*

We're so close I can almost taste his breath. Our lips are barely an inch apart. I'm not breathing.

*Screw it.*

My head tilts up instinctively, and that's it—I kiss him.

It's reckless, it's insane.

But it feels like the first real thing I've done in ages.

# Chapter 8

*Laura*

**HE CAN** kiss. *God*, can he kiss.

It's like he's read the manual on my mouth, written it, and then set it on fire. Maybe it's the whiskey's fault, lending him talents, but as his tongue tangles with mine, I know no bourbon's that good.

His hand's firm on my jaw, guiding me into a kiss that's all heat and hunger. His lips are soft, but the rest of him is all hard muscle. He's got me in a grip that says he's not letting go anytime soon, like I'm the oasis he's been dying to find in his personal desert.

I feel his hand locked on my back, as if he's afraid I'll bolt. Maybe I should. He's holding me like I'm the answer to questions I'm not sure I want to ask.

Despite the cold logic in my brain, my body's melting into his. I hate that I've craved this—his taste, the pressure of his mouth, the scrape of his stubble. I tiptoe up, fingers weaving through the hair at the nape of his neck, pulling him closer.

His growl vibrates from his chest to mine, a sound that sends pleasure spiraling down to my toes. As I let out a tiny whimper, his grip tightens, his hand slipping up to claim my neck, his thumb resting just below my ear, a silent command of possession.

Fuck, this man's got me twisted up inside more than any pretzel I've ever seen. His kiss tastes like a warning—of chaos, of ruin, of raw desire so potent it should have its own name. My heart hammers, fighting for space in my chest with every labored breath I take.

And *oh, my God*, I want him more than I've wanted anything in a long time. It's maddening to admit, but I've been craving this since our eyes first locked.

*This is fucking insane. I don't even know him!*

Wrapped up in his arms, I'm like some heroine in a midlife-crisis romance novel. And there's a whole divorce and criminal charges waiting to happen once I track down that *dick, David*.

*I should stop this.*

But then there's this voice in my head, loud and clear: *Why the hell should yo*u?

It's like my body knows what it wants before I do. My hands splay on his chest as if I could actually push him away.

Spoiler alert: *I can't.*

The guy's built like a tank. I push against him with all I've got, trying to break the kiss, but it's like trying to move a skyscraper with sheer will.

"What are you doing, *kiska*?" His voice is a low rumble. Lips linger.

"Trying to push you away," I breathe out, but who am I kidding? My body's *not* on board with this plan, *not* one bit.

He looks down at my hands against his chest, a hint of amusement in his eyes. "Not working, is it?" His expression is all cocky confidence, a smile that screams trouble.

And then, just like that, I'm air, I'm nothing—he's got me lifted against him, and we're moving. I can feel the cold bite of the night against my legs as he secures the coat around me, and for a second, I'm grateful—until I see where we're headed.

"Put me down!" I demand, my heart racing as he strides across the road toward Hotel V, a luxurious boutique hotel that looks like a room costs more than my yearly rent. It stands opposite Club V, a beacon of opulence and sin.

"Little firecracker," he murmurs, his breath warm against my hair. "It's too late."

"Too late for what?" My voice is a husky whisper, lost in the whirlwind of his presence.

He chuckles, his eyes dark pools of desire as he looks down at me. "I changed my mind; you're not going home tonight."

"But you said—"

I try to argue back, but he cuts me off. "Little firecracker," he says, and it's like a shot to the heart. "You should've thought of that before playing with matches."

My whole body goes on high alert, every nerve ending firing up. I feel a flush creep over my skin, my pulse races, and I hate how my body's betraying me—how it's responding to his words.

"Let me go. I'm serious," I insist, even as my voice cracks.

"I'm serious, too. You're mine now," he says with a possession that should scare me but instead sends a thrill down my spine. My cheeks are on fire, and I can feel that heat spreading, coiling low in my belly.

I squirm again, desperation lending me strength, but he's unyielding. "Victor," I warn.

"Stop fighting," he commands, and I freeze, his words striking me dumb. "You've got to learn to be a good little girl, or I'll have to spank that tight little pussy until you cum."

"Oh, my God!" I can't help the exclamation that slips out. I mean, who says that?

I stay still nonetheless, my eyes wide, my heart pounding out of control. "Good girl," he murmurs with approval, kissing my forehead.

"*Victor*!" I manage to say, my voice a mix of indignation and something dangerously close to desire.

"Yes, that's it, little firecracker. Soon, you'll be saying my name just like that, but for a whole different reason."

In my head, a million sirens are wailing, telling me this is insane, this is not me. I'm the woman who makes lists, who plans, who certainly doesn't get swept up by some… some dangerously magnetic guy. Yet here I am, carried like a doll by a man who's threatening to spank me.

And the craziest part?

It makes me horny as hell.

---

It turns out he *is* Russian.

Victor sweeps through the doors of Hotel V. The doorman's swift greeting, "Mr. Morozov," barely registers as I'm carried like a sack of rebellious potatoes into the hotel.

*Yep, he's definitely a VIP.*

The hotel's interior hits me like a swanky, velvet-lined hammer. Plush red carpets that probably cost more than my apartment, walls that seem to have been kissed by King Midas himself, and golden sconces casting a light so sultry it feels like it's undressing me.

He skips the front desk like it's not even there, heading straight for the elevator. I'm in his arms, light as a rag doll, while he strides through his turf. The staff's quick, wary glances tell me everything—this is his show.

He punches the penthouse button like it's an old habit. Do they just give penthouse access to anyone who's tall, dark, and scary?

Or is this like, his standard Friday night routine? Elevator rides to the penthouse with the flavor of the week?

Something else stirs in my gut—jealousy? No way, he's practically a stranger.

Questions bubble up, but they're on ice for now. I'm stuck to him, the heat of his body making all the looming doubts take a backseat.

But, oh God, what am I even thinking?

This isn't just crossing the line; this is catapulting over it. And still, his warmth, his scent, it's like a drug, and I'm embarrassingly tempted to take another hit. My body is betraying every rational thought with its traitorous longing.

"Victor," I say again, trying to infuse some kind of reprimand into my voice, but it comes out more like a whisper, a plea. It's ridiculous, I know. I should be fighting, arguing, demanding to be put down. Instead, I'm melting, and I hate myself a little for it.

The elevator dings, snapping me back to the present.

We're here, wherever *"here"* is.

And despite every screaming neuron in my brain, I can't deny the thrill that courses through me.

# Chapter 9

*Laura*

**I HEAR** his breathing.

A deep inhale and exhale.

The sound of a man in control. So close to me that I can feel his breath on my neck.

"Victor," I challenge, my voice a mix of defiance and an involuntary quiver, "where have you taken me?"

"To my penthouse," he replies, his voice a smooth, dark timbre that somehow makes the penthouse's opulence seem pale.

I pull in a breath, matching his control, trying to assert my own. The penthouse is all shadows and whispers of luxury, the kind that's spoken about in hushed, envious tones. The dim light plays tricks on the eyes, and every surface it touches seems to hum with silent promises.

I'm breathless, but not from fear. There's an energy here, crackling like the prelude to a storm, and it's infectious.

"This is your place?" I manage to ask, my voice coming out steadier than I expect.

A ghost of a smile plays on his lips. "One of them," he says, and the casual arrogance in his tone irks me, intrigues me.

*His penthouse?*

*Who the hell is this man? Hotel V belongs to him?*

My brain does a quick 180. *Duh, Laura.* "V" for Victor. *Of course.*

I can feel the weight of his gaze, heavy with intent, as if he's trying to read my every thought.

"You always bring your... guests here?"

"Shhhh. Curiosity can be dangerous, little firecracker. Best to leave it at the door."

Still carrying me, I feel his strong grip on my body as he drops me onto the wide leather couch.

I'm watching him, holding my breath, entranced, as he undoes his shirt buttons with an ease that's too much like the guys from the pages of my favorite steamy romances.

Sprawled on the sofa, I'm propped on my elbows, legs splayed like I'm prepped for a surprise pap smear, and my "doctor" is a stranger with a dangerously sexy vibe, smoldering eyes, and a presence that fills the room with raw heat.

Evidently, my mind's gone AWOL.

"Show me your tight little pussy, *kiska*." he growls.

I watch Victor rise between my legs like a warrior god, his strong thighs pressing against mine.

"Ex-excuse me?" I blink, stunned. "You didn't actually just say that?"

My mouth twitches, about to spit out a biting comeback. But as my eyes lock with his—so serious, no trace of jest—the words just hang there.

*Damn. He's dead set on seeing my vajayjay.*

"Wh-?" I barely manage, the urge to laugh now choked into a tight gulp.

"I told you, *kiska*," he puts a finger on my lips, "that you *owe* me." Then he kneels in front of me. He slides my dress up, pushing it further apart with his rough hands that blaze a path of fire across my body, up to my all-too-willing pussy.

"No more questions. Let me see what you are hiding there," he says, gruff and to the point. I'm taken aback, blinking in shock.

*Not a chance I'm letting this happen.*

"Just because you saved me earlier doesn't mean I owe you anything," I start, trying to sound bold, but my voice quivers. Victor's response is immediate, flipping my panties aside. His thumb presses against my clit, sending waves of unexpected pleasure surging through me. I gasp, my resolve wavering under his expert touch.

His intense gaze burns into me as his fingers teasingly brush against my wet folds. I whimper at the touch, wanting him to go further but also wanting to savor every moment of anticipation.

*What the fuck is happening to me?*

He's stroking my throbbing clit with his thumb, a slow and taunting rhythm that drives me wild. I can't resist giving in to the pleasure, even though I know it's wrong.

*Okay, I am letting this happen.*

I can't resist anymore, and I give in to the pleasure he's offering me. "Oh, fuck!" I gasp.

His voice is rough with desire as he says, "This is all mine." Slowly, he slips a finger inside of me,

"Oh… God." The movement draws a soft moan from my lips. My body trembles as he teases my sensitive nub, skillfully teasing and penetrating me until I'm soaking wet and swinging my hips, begging for more.

"I know what you want, *kiska*. If you ask so nicely, I'll leave no inch of your body untouched. I'll lap and feast on your wet cunt, then fuck it mercilessly. And if you're a good girl, I may even spank that sweet ass before fucking it."

My heart thunders against my rib cage at the thought. Never had I ever imagined a man being so bold and explicit with me.

His words are so direct, so unashamedly filthy, it's shocking. Yet, my body reacts, craving more. I'm shaking, torn between shock and an arousal so intense it's almost painful.

My mind is screaming that this is wrong, but my body betrays me. I'm melting under his touch, unable to deny the mounting desire. "Victor," my voice is a breathless whimper, "please…"

He grins, a predatory look in his eyes. "That's it *kiska*. Now, let's see how much you can take."

As he adds another finger, my body clenches around him, pulling him deeper. The rhythm he sets is relentless, driving me toward the edge. I clench my eyes shut, trying to escape the reality of what's happening, but it's futile.

Apparently, I've lost the plot.

"I-I don't do one-night stands," I manage to get out, my voice a jumble.

"Except, this isn't just a one-night stand," he counters, and every thought that comes after it is drowned out by the overwhelming sensation of wanting more.

*Wh-what does he mean?*

"Fuck... this... this is a mistake," I whisper. Trying to convince myself that it is true. But my body's not buying it; it's screaming, "Yes!"

The slick noises of my wetness echo in my ears like thunder as his fingers pump in and out, and further and further inside of me.

"But you want *this*," he asserts. "You want me to make you come." His words hang in the air, and in an instant, my G-string is swiftly removed in a single, forceful motion.

"Umm... no..." I open my eyes again and see him on his knees before me.

He's untamed, a savage sort of gorgeous that shouldn't exist.

Our gazes clash, his eyes catching the moonlight, fierce like a wolf's. *God*, he is too beautiful. It doesn't make sense.

Yet, here he is, a total stranger, and here I am, a complete wreck.

*This is crazy. I shouldn't...*

*But damn, I want to. I want him to make me come.*

"Don't feed me lies, little firecracker," he growls, a predatory glint in his eye. "Or I'll have to teach you a lesson." Before I can utter a sound, his thumb rubs my clit side to side faster.

A third finger joins. Pushing deeper, creating an almost suction effect that draws out all the juices clinging there. As another wave of pleasure washes over me, I sob uncontrollably.

For the first time ever, I don't know what to think. There's no room left for rational thought.

"Say it, or I won't let you come." His fingers move slower and slower as my hips instinctively rock against him, grinding for something more. "Say what you want, Laura."

"Alright, you win! I need you to make me come, okay? Just do it, please…"

*Good Lord, Laur, I had no idea you were so starved for action.*

"Good girl." He chuckles wickedly as he starts to move his dexterous fingers inside me, pushing higher until I feel my heart pounding in my throat and a red-hot liquid desire gathering deep within.

"Oh, oh, I… I am so close!" I moan. The warmth of his hand is against my pulsing heat.

"Let it go, Laura," he orders, his fingers thrusting deeper, hooking to stroke a secret spot that's all new to me. A tide of pleasure crashes over me as he amps up the pressure right on that magic spot.

"Fuck. Fuck. Fuck… I am…!" Waves of sensation crash over, pulling at something deep inside me, dragging it out… out… until finally it bursts forth from beneath—an orgasm so intense I lose track of myself in its wake.

Removing his fingers, he licks hungrily at my juices like some kind of wild beast, savoring every drop.

"You come so hard, *kiska*," he purrs, "but this is only the beginning…"

# Chapter 10

*Laura*

**HOLY FUCKING** hell.

I have never felt such intensity before, and I don't know how to process this newfound pleasure. I'm lying back on the sofa, still reeling from the shock of that mind-blowing orgasm.

*And...that's just his fingers doing the work.*

I'm dizzy with wanting more.

Every cell in me craves him. I watch him as he stands proudly over me, the room's dim light casting him in an almost holy glow.

He peels his shirt away; spectacular muscles roll across a broad chest and shoulders that look chiseled from stone. Runic symbols twist about his biceps like serpents caught in an eternal battle.

"Holy shit," I mutter under my breath, feeling completely entranced by his body.

"You like what you see?" he teases, and I can't even snap at him because, holy hell, he's a walking, talking piece of art.

"I hate to admit it, but yes." I roll my eyes playfully, trying to maintain some semblance of control.

"Good. Because I plan on making you crave more, *krasivyy*." His hand cups my cheek, and his thumb strokes my lips teasingly.

I grab a fistful of his hair and pull him down for a kiss that is filled with heat and need. It's like we're both starving for each other's touch.

When we finally break apart, panting and dizzy, a sense of familiarity washes over me. It's as if this is what I've been missing all along.

"I... I don't usually do this kind of thing," I blurt out, feeling the need to justify myself somehow.

"Well, lucky for you, you do now," he whispers huskily before slipping two fingers into my mouth, and I eagerly suck on them.

In that moment, there's no need for words. Our eyes are locked, and we both understand exactly what we want from each other.

Fuck it. I deserve this. And he deserves to be repaid in the same way.

I smile, feeling a surge of pleasure as his fingers move deeper into my mouth.

Yes. I definitely do.

*I want to get even.*

*Fuck it.*

My mind is a tempestuous tornado of pent-up rage fueled by the searing pain and ruthless betrayal inflicted by my deserting husband. Or perhaps it was the intoxicating whiskey shots igniting a burning hunger to break free. And then he appears, a magnetic stranger with a tempting offer to leave it all behind… and I am helpless against his seductive charm.

"Hmm…" Victor unleashes a guttural growl, his eyes wild with primal desire as I hungrily suck and lick his fingers, my mouth watering with anticipation.

I look at him with longing, knowing what's to come. He pulls his fingers from my mouth and plunges them into me without a moment's hesitation. A gasp escapes my lips as pleasure courses through me like an electric shock. Arching my back, I moan in response to his touch.

"Oh… yes," I moan against his lips as he kisses me again. His fingers continue their dance inside my wet pussy. Driving me wild with desire.

"That's it, *kiska*," he whispers huskily in my ear. Suddenly, he moves lower, his lips and tongue exploring every inch of my body as he hungrily yanks off my bra.

His eyes fixate on my exposed breasts, filled with unbridled lust. "I can't get enough of your tits," he groans before grabbing one roughly.

"Uhhhh… Yes." A surge of pleasure washes over me, and I writhe beneath him, unable to contain the sounds of ecstasy escaping my lips.

I'm stunned, crazy horny, and buzzed.

"God, yes," I moan, thrusting against his fingers as he hungrily suckles at my neck. "Harder!"

He grins wickedly and digs his nails into my sensitive nipple, twisting it until I cry out in ecstasy. My thighs tremble with need as he expertly works me over.

"You like that?" he taunts, his voice dripping with lust.

"Yes, yes. Fuck, I'm so close." And I am drenched and desperate for him to take me completely.

"You're so wet for me. Yes. Come for me," he growls in my ear as his fingers thrust deeper, harder, and faster inside of me.

"Fuck... Oh... fuck!" I yell out and my nails scratch down his back, leaving behind angry red marks. But he doesn't give a damn, and neither do I.

"Oh God, yes!" I scream, my body convulsing as wave after wave of intense pleasure crashes through me. My vision blurs as I lose control, my chest heaving and my heart racing so fast I think it might burst.

I've never come so easily with anyone, but with Victor it's like he knows all the secret places to touch and tease until I'm writhing beneath him. His weight pins me down, but instead of feeling trapped, I feel safe—I can't help but compare him to David—cold and distant in bed.

"Tell me," he growls again, as his fingers continue their relentless pace inside of me, "what desires are clouding your thoughts?"

My mind races with conflicting thoughts and emotions, but all I can manage to say is "Revenge." The word drips with venom and longing at the same time.

"Revenge?" he repeats with a smirk playing on his lips. And before I can even process what's happening, he leans down to capture my nipple between his teeth. The sensations crash over me like waves, pushing me closer and closer to the edge.

"I want revenge," I pant out between moans and gasps. But deep down, I know it's not just revenge I want—it's him. All of him.

"Fuck!" I scream. I scream in frustration, my voice cracking with pent-up desire. I need him inside of me.

"Be careful, *kiska*," he growls, his breath scorching as he leans closer to me. "In my world, revenge is a dangerous game—it can destroy you just as easily as it destroys your target."

I gasp as he starts licking and biting down on my nipple, the line between pleasure and pain blurring into one pulsing sensation.

"Fuck."

"Fuck."

His fingers plunge inside me, filling me up.

"I... I will have what I... deserve," I moan as his fingers tease my nipple, making it harder and harder while fueling my desire.

My heartbeat races with adrenaline and lust as I whisper, "Partly," knowing that my intentions are driven by the betrayal of my husband's infidelity and the loss of my store. But in this moment, with Victor, there is a sense of solace.

"What do you really want, Laura?" His voice is steady, but his eyes are wild with desire. I lock eyes with him and declare fiercely, "I want to feel alive again. To forget everything else." My words pour out like a torrent of emotion and pent-up longing.

"And... you want me," he states confidently, spreading my folds and gently teasing my clit with his fingertips. "You want me to fuck your horny little cunt."

"Y-yes," I gasp uncontrollably, unable to deny the truth as it spills from my lips. "I need you to fuck me," I beg shamelessly, consumed by the overwhelming urge to feel him inside me.

Victor's eyes turn wild, like a beast's been let loose. He's got this wicked smirk, like he knows he's about to cause some real trouble. "Is that so?" he says. With a devious grin, Victor ravages my mouth, igniting electric sensations all over my body. He frantically rips off my dress in a frenzy and parts my legs wider, his lips traveling down to my throbbing pussy.

"*Blyad*," he mutters against my wet pussy.

"Fuck, yes." As his mouth devours my exposed pussy with reckless abandon, I cry out in a mix of pain and pleasure. His tongue plunges deep inside me, lapping at me with insatiable hunger. And his skilled fingers thrust and curl inside me, driving me closer to the edge of ecstasy.

"Oh, God." I cling onto his shoulder, my nails digging into his skin as I surrender to the intense sensations wracking my body.

With three fingers still buried inside me, he twists and pinches my nipple, adding a new layer of electrifying pain to the pleasure pulsing through me. And instead of easing up, he pulls my hips up higher, forcing me to grind into his mouth as I reach climax.

Just when I think I can't take any more, he halts his movements and delivers a series of sharp slaps to my throbbing clit. Each one sends waves of agony and ecstasy through me until I can no longer hold back.

"Fuck, yes, fuck!" I scream and moan uncontrollably.

Victor commands with a possessive growl, "Come for me, *kiska*. Let the whole city hear who you belong to." And with that final command, I surrender completely to his dominance, lost in a sea of pleasure and pain.

*Victor.*

"Yes, Victor, yes…" I scream his name. And I cum on his fingers.

"That's my good girl. Ask for me to spank your ass and make you come again."

"Span- spank me," I barely manage to whisper, my voice trembling with anticipation.

Victor's eyes glint with a mix of desire and command. "Beg for it, *kiska*. Say *'please.'*"

As soon as I do, he flips me onto my stomach and begins spanking me hard and fast, alternating between each cheek while I grind my breasts against the sofa.

A gasp of delight escapes my lips, turning into a tremulous, ecstatic sob as I spread out my hands and grip tightly onto the soft leather. "Oh, fuck!"

Suddenly, he stops and plunges his fingers deep inside of me, grinning as he feels my dripping arousal. "I'm going to fuck this tight pussy of yours until it's screaming," he rumbles, his voice thick with desire.

"Please," I gasp in response, feeling my walls clench around his fingers in anticipation.

*I had no idea that raunchy talk could be such a turn-on for me.*

"Ask for it properly," he commands.

"Please! Please fuck me! I need you to fuck me!" I beg desperately.

Hearing me plead like that drives him wild.

Without hesitation, he aligns himself at my back. With a firm grasp on my hips, he pulls me onto all fours and unzips his pants. His cock springs out, fully erect and glistening with pre-cum, beckoning me closer.

"Is this what you want, Laura?"

"Yes," I gasp at the size of his cock. "I want… want your cock inside of me."

"Say please, Laura." He reaches over to the nightstand and retrieves a condom, sliding it on his hard cock with practiced ease. I can hardly contain my desire as he teases me with his length against my clit.

"Please," I beg, my body craving his touch.

Smacking my ass with his throbbing cock, he says, "This is what you do to me."

I moan in response, already feeling the familiar ache between my thighs. "Please, yes, please," I whimper, needing him inside me. He obliges, positioning himself between my legs. I can feel my arousal dripping onto my thighs as I arch up to meet him.

"Look at you, so fucking wet." With a husky groan, he enters me, filling me completely.

"Ah!" I jolt, caught off guard.

"You're mine, *kiska*," he reminds me in between thrusts, claiming me with each powerful movement.

My body is soaked in sweat as he grabs my waist, thrusting into me with a primal force. I can feel my orgasm building, bubbling just beneath the surface, and I know it won't be long until I explode again.

"Victor, yes, yes! Fuck, yes." Lost in the pleasure of being taken by him, I moan his name over and over.

He leans down to whisper in my ear, his hot breath fanning over my neck. "You like it rough, don't you, Laura?" he growls.

*No, I shouldn't... But I never knew I liked it this intense.*

"Yes," I moan, unable to form any coherent words as pleasure overtakes me.

With a guttural growl, he grabs my breasts and squeezes them with bruising force. His fingers twist my nipples until they throb with pain while he relentlessly pounds into me, his cock filling every inch of my insides.

"Oh, my God, I'm so close..." My body is on fire, teetering on the edge of another earth-shattering orgasm as he thrusts harder and deeper.

He responds by slamming into me with such force that my body rattles against the sofa.

"Fuck," he groans, reaching around to rub circles on my clit with his thumb. The added sensation pushes me over the edge, and I scream out in ecstasy.

His thrusts become almost frenzied, each one hitting a new spot inside of me that sends sparks shooting through my veins. I can't hold back the intense waves of pleasure that crash over me, and I feel a burst of wetness pulsing within me.

"You're so fucking wet," he growls and keeps thrusting with a ferocity that matches my own desire. "I can't get enough of you."

"Oh, God," I cry out. My mind goes blank as he takes me to new heights of pleasure.

"You're so delicious," he pants as he plunges his hard cock into me, slamming into me relentlessly, pounding against my body until my insides feel bruised and broken. *But* I fucking love it.

"Fuc-fuck!" I sob. "Fuck yes, Victor."

His hand glides up my side, caressing the curves of my ribs before cupping and squeezing my breast again. My nipple hardens under his touch as he pinches and pulls at it.

"Oh... fuck...!" I gasp in pain and pleasure.

*Fuck! Why does this feel so good?*

"I've wanted you since the moment I saw you." He reaches between us and starts fondling my swollen clit before spanking it, making me writhe with pleasure. The zipper of his pants rubs against my ass with every thrust of his hips, adding a delicious level of pain to the pleasure.

"God, you feel amazing," he moans, squeezing my breast before pinching my nipple roughly. I whimper in ecstasy, begging for more.

"Please... Yes, please."

"You like that?" he asks breathlessly as he continues to pound into me.

"Yes!" I cry out. "Do it again!"

He smirks and obliges, thrusting harder and faster until we're both on the brink of release.

"You're better than I ever imagined," he gasps, his words becoming rougher as he nears his climax.

"Mmm," I groan, too dazed to talk. With each thrust, he grunts in my ear, and I can feel myself getting closer to the edge. The sound of our bodies slapping together fills the room as I arch my back, begging for him to give me more.

Suddenly, it hits me like a freight train, a wave of pleasure coursing through my body as I come, while he's still pumping into me, grunting and cursing under his breath until he finally reaches his own release and empties himself inside of me.

He pulls out; I can feel a rush of wetness escape from me and hear him say one final word "*Blyad.*"

# Chapter 11

*Laura*

**SPRAWLED OUT,** naked, and exposed.

I'm a hot mess—literally. Sweat, cum, and ecstasy coat me, pleasure and guilt mixing in a bizarre cocktail.

All the anger and fear that were eating at me seem to have been wiped clean… until Victor's casual bombshell shatters the moment

"We broke the rubber," he announces as if he's just commenting on a slight change in the weather.

"We… What?" I gingerly touch the sticky aftermath on my pussy in disbelief.

My heart takes a nosedive, plummeting hard.

So much for the drunken bliss and the remaining glow of our earth-shattering romp.

*Fucking great, just great.*

On top of a runaway cheating husband and my finances going down the drain, now I've got a broken condom to top my list of "Life's Latest Disasters."

Victor stands there, looking as composed as ever, assessing the situation.

"Well, that's inconvenient," he says, infuriatingly calm.

Scrambling for some dignity, I sit up. "Inconvenient? It's a freaking disaster!" Tears well up unbidden. "Oh, God. What if I get pregnant?" Another panic strikes.

*Shit! I've missed a couple of birth control pills. There's been too much going on, one crisis after another—totally slipped my mind!*

He does this thing with his mouth, almost a smirk. "Ever heard of the morning-after pill?"

"Oh, sure, you're the go-to guy for contraception advice now?" I snap, my eyebrows arching in disbelief.

*Oh God, what have I gotten myself into?*

*Stupid, so stupid.*

Panic rises in my throat. "You've probably been with… God knows how many women. What if you've got something? What if I end up with AIDS?" The words tumble out.

Victor's eyebrows knit together in a mix of annoyance and amusement, running a hand through his hair. His half-naked form exudes a raw masculinity that's impossible to ignore. The room smells like a mix of our scents, a heady combination of sweat and the faint traces of his cologne.

*Why does he have to be so ridiculously good-looking?*

*Fucking hell, Laura. Stop it.*

Victor doesn't flinch, looking at me with a calm, assertive air. He firmly lifts my chin, making me look at him. "You're overreacting," he says, his voice flat, controlled. "I'm clean, Laura. No STDs, no AIDS."

"How can you be so sure?" My voice cracks under the strain.

"Because, Laura, I do my check up regularly." He raises an eyebrow, a flicker of disbelief crossing his face as he runs a hand through his hair again as if he can't quite believe he has to explain this.

"And how do you know I don't have anything?" I'm barely holding it together now.

He looks at me, his gaze firm but secretive. "I know everything about you, *Laura Anne Thompson*."

*What the hell is this? Am I in some kind of twisted movie?*

"How? How do you know my name?" My voice is a shaky whisper.

His tone is even, almost casual. "I make it my business to know."

*Oh, my God, Laura, what have you gotten yourself into?*

I'm frantically scanning the room, the full weight of what's happened crashing down on me. Here I am, butt-naked. My red dress is in shreds, looking more like a crime scene than an outfit.

My eyes dart to my handbag. Maybe I should just grab my phone and get out of here.

*Naked? Great, just great. How do I get out of this one?*

"Take it easy, Laura," he says calmly, his eyes seemingly dissecting my every thought. "You'll stay here tonight," he states, his authority unmistakable in his tone.

"No way," I say, my voice quivering. "I'm heading home."

"You're not going back home, not a chance…" It's like he's tapped into my mind. "You're safe here in my bed." Without warning, he scoops me up and strides over to this huge, extravagant bed. He drops me onto it, and I can feel the softness of the sheets against my bare ass.

"But I- I can't stay…" I try to protest, but his piercing gaze silences me. He smirks, his eyes dark with desire and control.

"Be a good girl and do as you're told, or there will be consequences," he warns in a low, dangerous voice. His domination is palpable, and I can't help but press my lips together in submission.

*Jeez, he's like a dog with a bone.*

"Look, I'm sorry about the damn condom," Victor throws in, his tone rough yet oddly apologetic. It's enough to stop me mid-thought.

His gray eyes lock with mine, and there's a warmth there that unexpectedly makes my stomach churn. Words try to form, but they're stuck somewhere between my brain and my mouth.

"Stay here, Laura." He's got this cooing tone now, like he's trying to calm a spooked animal. Weirdly, it's working. I'm feeling this odd sense of safety, even though everything inside me screams that I shouldn't.

Part of me wants to argue, to yell at him or throw my handbag at his too-perfect face.

But this is my fault—going out, wearing that dress, kissing this guy who screams "bad news" in every possible way.

"Stupid. I am just—" I start.

"Horny and lonely," he interjects, cutting me off. "And now, a little scared. It happens."

My eyes might be rolling in irritation, but I can't ignore the sight of Victor's erect, dripping cock on full display.

*When did he strip off his pants? How is he rock-hard again?*

*Damn! Focus, Laura.*

"I... I'll need to clean up." I push these thoughts away, standing up abruptly to stride into the bathroom. I dart past him before my body has a chance to betray me again.

Slipping into the bathroom, I'm hit by the sheer luxury of it.

The full-length mirror throws back my reflection, and there it is—a mark, bold as sin, on my breast, a souvenir from Victor's fervent grip. My eyes flicker upwards, catching sight of a chandelier lamp throwing soft light across the room, lavish and totally over-the-top.

*Who the hell is this guy?*

Can't think because I'm beyond exhausted at this point; all I want to do is pass out right here.

Setting my feet on the cool, luxurious tiles, I flick on the shower. Instantly, a rush of warm water envelops me. The water beads on my hard nipples, a sharp reminder of what just went down. I can't help but catch my blurry reflection in the mirror, covered in suds, looking back at a woman I barely recognize—one who's just had the most mind-blowing sex of her life. Was I really that desperate, that needy? But something about him makes me feel like a horny teenager.

I run my hands over my body, washing away the evidence, lingering a moment too long between my legs.

The reality of it all hits me again—I let this happen, with a stranger, no less.

A guy I'll probably never see again. A mix of regret and satisfaction washes over me, just like the shower's spray. I close my eyes.

Then, out of nowhere, I sense it—this overwhelming masculine energy closing in on me. It's unmistakable, raw, and powerful. I feel Victor's looming presence behind me. His big, intimidating body towers over mine.

"Fuck, Victor," I gasp, still caught off guard by his boldness. "Can I have some privacy?"

Ignoring my protest, he presses himself against me. I can feel the heat radiating from his body as his large hands wrap around me, trapping me in his grasp. His hard length throbs upward, so long and thick that it reaches the small of my back.

*Why the hell does this drive me crazy?*

Lowering his head, he whispers in my ear. "Let me show you," he growls, pressing his fingers against mine to my throbbing clit. His fingers take control, rubbing in circles, faster and harder until I feel like I might explode. Then he plunges one of his fingers into me alongside mine, intensifying the pleasure beyond anything I could have imagined or experienced.

"Oh... my God," I moan, leaning back against his broad chest as he continues to expertly guide my hand.

"You can take it," he insists, his hot breath tickling my ear.

"God, Victor," I whimper weakly. He lifts my chin with his fingers and crashes his lips onto mine. Water drips down his muscular back as our kiss intensifies, his hand gliding down and expertly fondling and tickling my nipple, driving me wild as I pound on his strong fingers.

"Oh, fuck," he groans, feeling my body tense and spasm under his skilled touch. "You're so fucking sexy," he whispers hoarsely.

"I can't... I can't take it." I gasp as Victor's lips muffle my cries of pleasure.

"Yes," Victor taunts, his fingers moving in and out of me with a brutal speed and force. "You like that, don't you?"

"Yes... fuck, fuck, fuck, yes." I moan uncontrollably, completely lost in the ecstasy as he relentlessly finger-fucks me. "Yes... yes, oh God," I cry out in pleasure. "You're going to make me come again," I choke out, barely able to form coherent words as he groans in response.

"Come for me, Laura."

I can feel his rock-hard shaft pressing against my lower back, aching to be inside of me.

With a primal growl, he declares, "You are mine. Laura. I want to ravage every inch of your body until you're screaming my name." His skilled fingers slide in and out of me faster, igniting an inferno of pleasure throughout my entire being.

Guilt floods through me as I remember my wedding vows and the promise I made to David. "I… I'm married," I pant out suddenly, trying to hold on to any shred of rational thought. But at this point, it doesn't matter anymore…

"Are you sure?" he snarls, hitting my G-spot with his fingers.

"Fuck!" I curse as his fingers thrust inside me, my muscles clenching around them. "Wh- What do you mean?" I force a breath out, fighting to keep my thoughts clear.

"Be quiet now," Victor commands. I feel a primal lust emanating from him as he silences me with a harsh yank on my hair. "Do as you're told, my little firecracker." His hand tightens around my hip, pulling me closer to him. "Or else, you'll get the punishment you deserve."

My body responds immediately, the wetness between my thighs increasing as he teases and slides his hard length against my aching clit.

"God, you're so wet for me," he groans, pressing hot kisses along my neck. "You want this?" he taunts, teasingly rubbing himself against my entrance.

I nod desperately, needing him inside me. "Yes."

He smirks and slowly slides in, causing me to arch my back and moan. But just as quickly as I start to find my rhythm, he pulls out.

"Oh, come on," I whine. "Don't tease."

"I want you to feel every inch of me," he growls, his fingers curling around my rock-hard nipple and another hand relentlessly rubbing my throbbing clit.

Every nerve in my body feels electrified, begging for release. "Please... fuck me," I whimper, my frustration growing with each passing second.

"I love hearing you beg for my cock," he says with a sadistic smirk, using his other hand to slide the head of his hard cock through my wetness until it's slick and ready. Gripping my hips tightly, he thrusts inside me, filling me completely. I scream out his name, unable to contain the pleasure coursing through me.

"You like that? You like how I fuck you?" he grunts, thrusting deeper and faster into me.

"Mmhmm," I moan, arching my back and holding myself from slamming into the wet wall.

"Good girl. Now tell me who this tight little pussy belongs to," he demands harshly.

I try to speak, but all I can do is moan as he hits that perfect spot inside of me.

"Tell me," he demands again. I can barely think straight, let alone speak, but with each deep thrust and flick of his thumb against my sensitive clit, my body screams out for release.

"Please," I beg, my voice hoarse and desperate. "It's yours. All of me is yours."

I am his to take, his to use, and I revel in the pleasure and pain he inflicts upon me.

He grunts. "*Blyad*, you surprise me, little firecracker," he mutters. "Better than I ever imagined." His voice is coarse, and his breath is ragged. He's about to lose it. He slams into me a few more times before swearing in Russian.

"Drop to your knees. I want your mouth ready for me."

Letting go of me, he steps back and turns off the shower.

Gasping for air, I spin around to face him. With a vise-like grip on my hair, he forces me onto my knees and presses his throbbing cock against my lips. His voice is low and commanding as he orders.

"Suck it, swallow it all. And if you dare waste a single drop of my cum, you'll regret it."

I kneel in front of Victor, my mouth watering with desire as I take his throbbing cock eagerly between my lips. His groans of pleasure only fuel my hunger as I slowly lick along his length, savoring the taste of his pre-cum on my tongue. My hands grip tightly around him as I swirl my tongue around the head before taking him fully into my mouth.

"Mmm, you taste so fucking good," I moan between mouthfuls as he thrusts deeper into me, hitting the back of my throat with each stroke. I intensify the pressure of my sucking and stroke, making him groan and writhe against me.

"Fuck, you are perfect," he growls, his eyes locked on mine as I continue to worship his cock with my mouth. With each thrust, I feel him getting closer to the edge, and I know it won't be long until he explodes.

Feeling his cock twitch and throb in my mouth, I look up at him. And I give a final suck.

"I'm coming," he announces, his voice rough with desire as he releases himself into my waiting mouth. With one final deepthroat, I drink down every last bit of him.

# Chapter 12

*Victor*

**I'M STILL** reeling from her mouth, hot and wild around my cock.

*Blyad*, I'm craving more, feeling my balls tighten up with the thought of her. The urge to ditch this shit and dive back into bed with her is hitting me hard.

But fuck, Misha rings me up at the Devil's hour, right before I could get another round with her. Says we've snagged a rat, one of Ivan Vasiliev's sneaky bastards.

As I stride down to the den, my own personal hellhole, the air gets thicker, reeking of fear and sweat. The guards nod at me, their faces grim.

"Boss," they grunt, stepping aside.

I push open the heavy metal door, and the sound of dripping water and deep groans hit me. It's a fucking symphony to my ears. This place, with its dark corners and chains hanging from the ceiling, is where I deal with traitors.

Chained to the wall is the traitor. A once-trusted capo, now nothing but a rat. His face is a mess of bruises and blood, barely alive.

"Enjoying your stay, Fyodor?" I sneer.

The sound that comes out of him is a wet, gurgling mess, like a fish gasping for air on dry land. He's sobbing, blubbering, blood oozing from where his teeth used to be.

"Why? Can't speak?" I mock him.

Misha's handiwork is evident. Fyodor's face is a wreck. His right eye, swollen shut, looks like it's been worked over with a hammer. The bloodied floor tells a tale of teeth yanked out one by one.

His fingers are all broken, twisted in unnatural angles. Classic Misha—doesn't hold back, especially not with traitors.

We don't let rats like Fyodor live.

It's a sign of weakness, and weakness is something the Bratva can't afford.

"Son of a bitch, Fyodor. Fifteen million in shipment goods. Drugs, cash, and fucking loyalty," I spit the words at him.

His tears are streaming now, mixing with the blood and dirt on his face. "You let Ivan and his goons take a piece of us. That's not how we play." Rage boils in me, thinking of Laura, how I'm torn from her body because of this mess.

He's whimpering now, pleading.

I turn to the table, eyeing the knives. There's a range—from the slender stiletto, perfect for precise cuts, to the hefty cleaver, used for messier jobs. Each tells a story of the Bratva's dark deeds.

"Should I slice you up, feed you to the dogs, or maybe skin you slowly?" My fingers trace the cold steel of each knife.

Fyodor's plea comes out garbled, *"Pozhaluysta…"* He's begging, but it's too late for mercy.

I pick up the short knife, feeling its familiar weight.

"What did you think would happen, Fyodor? Betraying the Bratva is a death sentence." I press the blade against his ear and, with a quick motion, slice it off.

His scream pierces the dank air of the dungeon.

In the Bratva, betrayal is paid in blood and pain. Mercy is a weakness, and loyalty is the only currency.

But still, there are morons like Fyodor who think they can screw over the Bratva and not end up dead.

*Fucking idiots.*

Then Misha barges in, no fucking knock or anything, snapping me back to the harsh present.

"I've got bad news."

I don't want to hear bad news. "Talk to me about it later when—"

"Ksenia is here," he blurts.

*Chert poberi, what could Ksenia want at this hour?*

I spin around, my glare piercing through him. He's pointing behind me, but I'm too pissed to care. "Then tell her to f—"

"Hello, brother."

I wince.

That voice.

My sister.

The tension in the room thickens, and I turn, facing Ksenia. She stands there, all ice queen composure; her eyes, as sharp as daggers, hold a wolf-like power in their gray depths.

She smirks, crossing her arms. "You look like shit. Rough night?"

Ignoring the sounds of Fyodor coughing, crying, shitting, and pissing himself in fear, Ksenia strolls into the dungeon like she owns the place.

This hellhole, where our father used to slice enemies apart, is her playground. At forty-one, six years older than me, she looks at least a decade younger than her age. Ksenia has got this aura—dark, untouchable. Her chestnut hair is pulled back in a bun, her silver-gray eyes scanning the room like she's plotting a war.

"You always had a stomach for this, didn't you, Ksenia?" I remark, trying to mask my unease.

"Comes with the territory, little brother," she replies, her gaze landing on Fyodor. "So, this is the rat?"

I don't even bother asking how she knows. She just does. Always in the loop; that's Ksenia.

"Yeah, that's the rat," I say, keeping my voice steady despite the turmoil inside. "Misha caught him handing over shipment details to Vasiliev's crew."

Ksenia circles Fyodor like a predator assessing its prey.

Her eyes don't betray a thing, but I can't help but watch her closely as I mention Vasiliev. There's a history there, buried deep but not forgotten.

"Good. We need to send a message. Can't have rats thinking they can scurry around without consequences."

"I know the rules, Ksenia," I snarl, the memory of her and Ivan Vasiliev flashing through my mind. It's been over twenty years, but the thought still burns.

*Love? More like a cursed pisdec.*

She nearly threw everything away for him, even tried to elope. But our father caught wind of it, threatened to kill Ivan if she didn't leave him and marry Dmitry, the guy he had picked out.

*Daughters*? To our old man, they're just chess pieces, nothing more.

*Marrying for love*? In his world, that's a damn joke.

She was once young, naive. Now? Ksenia turned into a whole different beast.

"Was about to finish him off before you showed up," I continue, pushing the memories aside.

Ksenia strides up to Fyodor and grabs a knife off the tray, its blade catching the dim light.

"What a pity. You've been a good dog all these years, haven't you?" she taunts.

With a twisted smirk, she starts slicing into him. Fyodor's eyes widen in terror as she begins her work, each cut delivered with clinical precision.

His screams echo off the walls; the more he screams, the wider Ksenia's cold smirk grows.

I cringe watching this shitshow.

"Alright, Ksenia, cut it out…" I hiss.

Damn, I actually feel sorry for Fyodor. Ksenia's in a nasty mood today.

"You're turning this into a bloody mess," I snap quietly.

Dropping the knife, she wipes her bloody hands without a care. She grabs some masking tape, peeling off a strip with a sharp sound.

Without a hint of mercy, she tapes up his nose and mouth, smothering him. His body shakes desperately, trying to suck in air. Ksenia just watches, cold as hell, as Fyodor's struggles turn into spasms. His legs kick out, a pathetic last dance, and then he's just a lifeless heap.

I grunt, watching the scene unfold.

"Fuck's sake Ksenia. What's the emergency?" I ask through clenched teeth, pushing away any shred of feeling. "Please don't tell me you're here just to enjoy a kill," I say in frustration.

Ksenia turns to me, her eyes like chips of ice. "Relax, little brother, I am just doing the dirty work for you."

I'm not sure if I believe her. Ksenia's always been more ruthless than the rest of us, and I've seen her do worse without batting an eye.

She pauses, her face losing its usual edge. "It's Papa. They think he's had a stroke. He's finally caved and gone to the hospital."

My heart sinks, but I mask it with a scowl. "And...?"

"And," she adds, "he wants you married. ASAP. We need to keep the Bratva strong, Victor. You need to step up as the *Pakhan*..."

"I'm not fucking with that mess again," I spit out, pissed.

*Shit, the last time I talked to Papa, we were arguing about this very thing. Now, the old man's laid up in a hospital bed, and here I am, still stubborn as ever.*

Guilt gnaws at me, but I shove it down.

"Why the hell are we dragging this ancient crap around?" I snap. "Doesn't mean I have to marry some chick just to prove I'm a badass, Ksenia."

"Stop bitching, you knew this was your shit to deal with since you were shitting diapers," Ksenia fires back.

*Blyad, I hate it, but my sister is right.*

"And I think this time it's bad," Ksenia says, dead serious.

"What the fuck am I supposed to do about it?" I snap, pissed off and frustrated.

"There's a list of candidates. Choose, or we're all fucked," she states bluntly.

I rub my temple. "Candidates?"

She flicks a folded paper my way, and I catch it.

Misha's looking like he wants to be anywhere but here, his eyes flicking back and forth between us.

"Great," I mutter sarcastically. "Can't wait to see this parade of princesses."

Ksenia's smirk widens. "You'll get a kick out of them, I'm sure."

I scan the list, my face screwing up in disgust.

*Suka.*

"Anastasia Petrova? Her old man's a money-grubbing *sukin syn*. And Ekaterina Smirnov? That whole family's shadier than a night in Moscow."

Misha chimes in, trying to lighten the mood, "But hey, Ekaterina's got a hell of an ass, right?"

I shoot Misha a cold look, unamused.

"Victor, they're solid mafia blood," Ksenia argues, rolling her eyes.

*Fuck, my mind is consumed by thoughts of Laura and the slick, sweet pussy between her thighs.*

I toss the list aside. "This is all bullshit. I'm not tying myself to some power-hungry bitch family."

Ksenia's in my face now, her tone hard. "It's not your call. Papa's dying wish. Choose one and keep the Bratva strong."

"He is not dying." I scowl, feeling trapped. "*Chert voz'mi*, Ksenia. I'm a mob boss, not a fucking matchmaker.

She picks up the list, shoving it at me. "Man up, little brother. This is bigger than your dick. Do it for Papa, for the Bratva."

"Ksenia, if I am doing this, I am doing it my way."

"Do you have someone else in mind?" Her eyes pierce through me, searching.

I break her stare, looking at Fyodor's dead body. Blood drips everywhere, his life snuffed out like a candle. *Blyad*, if I don't get this sorted, we're in deep shit.

News spreads like wildfire here, and if other gangs catch wind that the old man, the *Pakhan*, is battling health issues, losing his strength, they'll see it as a weakness, a crack in our armor. Whether I like it or not, these traditions need to be adhered to.

Ksenia's got a point; the Bratva's riding on my fucking decisions now.

But hell, I'm not giving her the satisfaction of knowing she's hit the nail on the head.

"That's none of your business," I growl back at her.

Ksenia turns to leave the room but pauses at the door. "By the way, you have five days to decide who you're going to marry."

# Chapter 13

*Laura*

**BREAKFAST IS** an extravagant affair straight out of a glossy magazine, all thanks to Naomi, the young redhead who brought it in.

I'm digging into a fluffy omelet, rich with herbs and cheese, and some perfectly salty bacon on the side. Then there are these pancakes, soaking in maple syrup, topped with a melting butter blob—insanely delicious.

I chomp down on a heart-shaped melon slice.

"Mmm…" I can't help but moan, the taste so fresh, it's like it was just picked off the vine this morning.

I look around the room, my head still spinning from last night. What the hell was I thinking? The luxury around me feels surreal, like

I've stepped into someone else's life. Wrapped in this soft hotel robe, I feel out of place yet oddly regal.

No, not regal—more like Julia Roberts in "Pretty Woman," but without the hooker part.

I check the time. It's still early, not as early as when Victor left after washing me up, drying my hair—something no one's ever done for me—and tucking me into bed.

Then he gets a call, his face tightening up, all serious. Next thing I know, he's hastily throwing on his clothes, clearly annoyed.

"Don't go anywhere," Victor's whisper echoes in my ears. "If I don't see you here when I get back, you'll get your punishment."

"You can't keep me here; that is called kidnapping," I remember protesting, feeling his hands over my neck, his breath against my lips.

"Do as I say, Laura," he demands, his teeth grazing my nipple before he sucks it into his mouth, his tongue swirling around the sensitive bud.

"No," I gasp, my hands tangling in his hair as he sucks and licks at my nipple, sending jolts of pleasure straight to my core. I try to push him away, but my body betrays me, arching into his touch.

"You, little firecracker, are mine," he growls, his hands gripping my waist, pulling me closer.

"It's creepy when you keep saying that," I shoot back, rolling my eyes. But I'm clenching my pussy, responding to his touch with a maddening mix of frustration and desire. "And I'm not yours," I manage, my voice breathy and unconvincing even to my own ears.

He doesn't laugh. His stare is intense, unwavering. "Be a good girl, little firecracker," he warns, his fingers digging into my skin.

I meet his gaze head-on, defiant. "Not happening." The words are out before I can stop them, tumbling from my lips in a rush. "I'll never see you again, Mr. Victor Morozov."

Even as I say it, my heart sinks, a hollow ache settling in my chest. But I can't take it back now. I won't.

His eyes flash, something dangerous and possessive swirling in their depths. He leans in close, his lips brushing against my ear.

"We'll see about that, won't we, Laura?" His voice is a low rumble, a promise and a threat all in one.

I shiver, my pulse racing. I know I should push him away, should run as far and as fast as I can. But some traitorous part of me wants to stay, wants to see just how far this dangerous game will go.

God help me, but I'm not sure I'm strong enough to resist him. Not when he looks at me like that, touches me like that.

Like I'm his for the taking, and nothing in the world can stop him.

*Stop it, Laur. Stop this.*

Yeah, it's been wild and crazy. But it's time to dive back into my own chaos.

Then, suddenly, he flips me over. His hand comes down on my ass with a sharp smack that echoes in the room. It stings, burns even, and I can't help but let out a gasp, a mix of shock and something else, something heated.

"Don't think of leaving without my permission," he taunts, his voice low and dangerous.

I try to wriggle away, but he's too strong. "You can't just spank me into staying, you know."

Victor moves in close, his breath hot on my ear. "Perhaps I can, Laura."

And then he just stops.

He stands up straight, gives me one more heated look that makes my insides twist. Without a word, he storms out the door, leaving me a jumbled mess of anger, confusion, and a burning desire that I can't fucking ignore.

*Damn him.*

How long does he expect me to wait? A day? A year? Forever?

I decide to test my boundaries, to see if I'm actually free to leave. I walk to the balcony, taking cautious steps, half-expecting someone to stop me or a drone to buzz overhead with guns blazing. But nothing happens. The sky is clear, the sun warm on my skin.

Staring down at the city below, I'm hit with a sudden resolve.

"Screw this," I mutter to myself. "Who does he think he is?" I can't just stick around waiting for a hot, sexy, ass-spanking hotel owner, no matter how tempting that idea is.

I storm back into the room, ditching any lingering fantasies.

With a sharp *thwack*, I smack my face, jolting myself back to reality. No more getting lost in thoughts about that stranger's touch.

Naked, with only a hotel robe for cover. My phone's as dead as my bank account.

*Who cares if I look like a spa escapee?*

"Not happening again," I quietly assure myself, pretty sure that was the final chapter with him.

---

Stupid.

So fucking stupid.

Broken condom, hot dangerous stranger, and the best sex ever still don't justify this madness.

*What the hell was I thinking?*

Hauling the Hotel V robe back to my cramped apartment, I give it a long, hard stare. The soft fabric, emblazoned with that damn "V," taunts me. My heart skips a beat. *V for Victor.*

His cologne still clings to it, a faint but distinct reminder of him threading through my senses. Damn him.

*Get a grip, Laura.*

After a quick, squeaky shower, I'm back in my jeans and sweater—the usual Laura. Stepping out into the brisk air, I head for the nearest pharmacy.

The bell above the pharmacy door jingles as I enter. Behind the counter, there's Linda, with her ever-present knowing smile.

"*Plan… Plan-B*, please," I request, avoiding her gaze.

Linda's eyebrows shoot up in surprise, but she quickly masks it with a professional smile. "Here you go," she says, handing over the pill.

I just nod, slapping down the cash without another word. A hot wave of shame and guilt surges in my chest.

"Have a lovely day," I mumble, mustering every ounce of politeness before bolting out the door.

Back in my apartment, I throw the pharmacy bag on the table and glare at it. "Nice job, Laura," I grumble to myself.

Grabbing the morning-after pill, I gulp it down with a swig of water.

It's done.

My chest clenches, a raw, nagging ache. Three years and two days with David, and every damn time I brought up kids, he shut me down cold. Just like that.

Sometimes, I envy watching Ser and James. They've got it all—love, laughter, and little Lucas toddling around, tying them together in the cutest way possible. They're like a beacon of what true love and family should be, a stark contrast to the emptiness I feel with David.

*I should've seen it coming. That deceitful, backstabbing bastard.*

Shaking off thoughts of David, I pull my phone from its charger, the screen dark and lifeless until I power it up. The moment it comes to life, it's like opening a floodgate.

*Correction.* More like a hell's gate of digital chaos.

Messages and missed calls swarm the screen.

*God, what a mess.*

Missed calls from *UNKNOWN NUMBER* at 8.15 a.m., then again at 9.37 a.m., and 9.48 a.m. Who the hell is that persistent?

My fingers hover over the delete button, but curiosity wins. I leave them be for now.

Then, Mr. Henderson's name blinks back at me from the screen, a glaring reminder of the headache I'm about to face.

Sixteen missed calls from 6:35 a.m. to 10.55 a.m. from my landlord is not odd at all, the guy's got the patience of a toddler, but this time, I get why he's freaking out.

In my mind's eye, I see his face: mid-50s, skin like leather from too many years of scowling under the sun, and eyes that don't miss a trick. He's the kind of guy who'd charge you for breathing if he could. No love for late rent or fresh ideas to spruce up his decaying two-story monument to the past. He must've caught wind of the bookstore looking like a set piece from a ghost story.

Sorry, but I just can't handle his drama right now. I'll deal with him later. More missed calls and messages flood my screen. I let out a dry laugh.

*Laura Anne Thompson, girl, you're more popular than a celebrity in a scandal.*

I tap on Dad's texts, my fingers trembling with dread.

**Dad (7:24 a.m.): "Laura, what have you screwed up now?"**

**Dad (7:27 a.m.): "This is on you. Don't expect me to bail you out again."**

His words sting like a slap. I grit my teeth, feeling that familiar wave of resentment.

**Dad (7:31 a.m.): "Can't you do anything right? The bookstore was fine before you took over."**

**Dad (7:35 a.m.): "You're just like your mother, making a mess of things. I won't fix your blunders forever."**

I squeeze my eyes shut, trying to block out his harsh words. My breathing is ragged, each text a reminder of his constant criticism.

*No, not now. I can't deal with this now.*

I switch to Serena's messages, desperate for a shred of sanity.

**Gothic Goddess Ser (8.55 a.m.): "Lulu, where are you? Haven't heard from you since last night. Are you okay??"**

**Gothic Goddess Ser (9:12 a.m.): "Seriously, I'm starting to freak out here. *Worried face emoji* Please just text me back."**

Missed call from Gothic Goddess Ser at 9.13 a.m.

**Gothic Goddess Ser (9:35 a.m.): "Okay, now I'm imagining all sorts of terrible scenarios. Are you safe? *Anxious face emoji*"**

**Gothic Goddess Ser (10:03 a.m.): "Hey, if you hooked up with some hot billionaire and ran off to Paris, at least send a postcard! *Laughing face emoji*"**

*If only, Ser. If only my life was that kind of mess.*

**Gothic Goddess Ser (10:07 a.m.): "Lulu, if you don't text me back soon, I'm calling the cops. *Angry face emoji*"**

I glance at the clock. It's nearly 11:00 a.m.

**Gothic Goddess Ser (10:19 a.m.): "Alright, that's it. I'm coming over.** *Angry face with steam from nose emoji.* **And you better not be in Paris!"**

Missed call from Gothic Goddess Ser at 10.32 a.m.

I tap the screen to call Serena, and at the first ring, her voice blasts through both my phone and from just outside my door.

"Laura!" she yells, her voice a mix of concern and a drill sergeant's command. "Laura Anne Thompson!" The second call-out is even louder, accompanied by a series of frantic knocks that sound like a SWAT team's about to breach.

I can't help but crack a smile. I open the door, still clutching my phone.

There stands Serena, phone pressed to her ear, her other hand raised mid-knock like she's ready to break down the door.

"I'm right here, Ser," I say, half-laughing.

Her eyes widen in mock horror. "Thank God! I was about to call in a search party! Or worse, your dad!"

She barges in, still on the phone, now eyeing my apartment like she's expecting to find a secret passage or a hidden hostage.

"Ser, you can hang up now," I say, ending the call on my phone.

She dramatically presses "end call" and then turns to me, eyebrows raised. "You go MIA, miss calls and texts. What was I supposed to think? That you'd run off to Vegas to marry a Chippendale?"

"Sorry, I…" I pause.

Still in high gear, Serena strides over to my kitchen. She grabs a glass, filling it with water, her movements exaggerated, almost theatrical.

"Or worse, what if you got nabbed by a horny werewolf looking for his moonlit soulmate?" she quips, a mischievous glint in her eye, no doubt a spark from her latest paranormal romance.

Forcing a weak laugh, I shake my head. "Yeah, because my life's just a page out of one of your novels, right?"

Serena takes a dramatic sip of water, then places the glass down with a flourish. "With the way your luck runs? I wouldn't be surprised. So, spill it. What kind of trouble did you dive into this time?"

I shake my head, amused yet grateful for her concern. "Nothing so exciting, Ser. I just got drunk…"

*Sorry, Ser, but I'm not about to spill the beans on my fling with one of the sexiest humans I've met.*

Trying to change the subject. "How's Lucas?" I ask.

Serena gulps down the rest of the water as if she's just trekked through the Sahara. She switches to mom mode effortlessly. "Oh, the little guy's got the sniffles. James is doing the whole 'Daddy to the rescue' bit, playing astronauts. They're probably on a mission to Mars as we speak."

Now she's rummaging through my fridge, on the hunt for something edible. She pulls out an old pack of cheese slices, peeling one off, and popping it into her mouth like it's gourmet.

"I'm really sorry for bailing on you last night… Lucas was being super cl-clingy and…" Her voice trails off as her eyes lock onto my table. The cheese slice hangs forgotten from her fingers.

Serena's smile vanishes, replaced by shock. "Hang on… Lulu, is that what I think it is?" She points, mouth wide open.

"Oh, my God, is that a morning-after pill?"

# Chapter 14

*Laura*

**SERENA'S EYES** widen to the size of a full moon.

I bite my nails as I watch her gaze ping-pong between the Plan B packaging on the table and me. "Spill it, Lulu," she commands. "And don't you dare leave out any juicy details!"

I feel my cheeks heating up. "It's not what you think, Ser. I mean, it is, *but…*"

She interrupts, "You had unprotected whoopie with a stranger? That's so unlike you!"

I sink into the couch, feeling a mix of guilt and exhilaration. "I know, it was stupid, and now I'm freaking out."

My best friend plops down next to me, her expression a mix of shock and amusement. "Honey, this is more drama than my 'Moonlit Desires' series. I'm half-scandalized, half-impressed."

I wince. "But I'm still technically married to that slimeball David…"

She waves a hand dismissively. "That useless son of the gun? He's about as useful as a screen door on a submarine. Lulu, you deserve some fun."

I nibble my lip, torn between guilt and exhilaration. "I don't know, Ser. I feel like I'm crossing a line here."

She leans in, her eyes gleaming. "Crossing the line? Honey, you catapulted over it. And I'm here for it! Who's the mystery man? Anyone I know?"

I shake my head. "No, just… someone I met at Club V.

*Damnit. Victor Morozov. Why can't I shake him?*

One night, that's all it was. Barely even a blip in my life. But here I am, his name still rattling around in my head.

*It's stupid. Pointless. He's gone, and I'm here, and that's that. End of story.*

So why does it feel like there's a hole in my chest where he used to be? Why do I catch myself wondering where he is, what he's doing?

I can't do this. Can't let myself get caught up in something that was never real to begin with.

*It was one night. That's all. And now it's over.*

*Time to move on.*

I groan, burying my face in my hands. "I'm a mess, Ser. My store's gone, Dad and the landlord are on my butt, and now this…"

She wraps an arm around my shoulder.

"You're not a mess; you're just… well, human. And honestly, your guy radar could use a serious upgrade. It's like you've got a magnet for the 'bad luck' type."

I let out a snort. "Wow, Ser, with pep talks like that, who needs enemies?" I can't help but chuckle despite the chaos in my life. Serena always has a way of making light of even the darkest situations.

"But hey, at least you finally got laid after, what, a geological era?"

I grimace. "Eight months and twenty days, to be exact, long before David pulled his vanishing act. But who's counting."

"To be honest, I've always felt something was *off* with David…like a closed book."

I nod, feeling a surge of bitterness. "More like a book in a language I can't read. Always secretive, always distant."

"God, Ser, what if there was more to David? What if…?"

"What? You think he was into something shady?" Serena's eyes narrow, a detective-like glint in them. "Like what, already married with a family? Or smuggling diamonds?"

My stomach twists.

"I don't know about the smuggling diamonds… but now that I think about it, he did have a lot of 'business trips' that never added up." A chill runs through me as I recall that night. David, his face unreadable, lugging in a heavy suitcase, claiming it was just work stuff. But the way he avoided my eyes…

Serena grabs a cushion, hugging it to her chest. "Lulu, this is like something out of a crime novel. You think you were living with a criminal?"

My heart races, the pieces starting to fit together in a terrifying puzzle. Those late-night calls he whispered into, the strange friends who never stayed long.

"I-I just don't know, Ser. But…"

"Okay, let's not jump to conclusions." Serena reaches over, her hand gently squeezing mine. She locks eyes with me, an eyebrow raised in anticipation. "But seriously, Lulu, I'm dying to know about what happened to you last night! Was he at least hotter than a summer in the Sahara?"

No matter how grim things seem, Serena's got a gift for making everything feel a bit brighter and more bearable.

I sigh. "Hot doesn't even begin to cover it. But it was just a one-time thing. No strings attached."

Serena raises an eyebrow. "Famous last words. Watch, this will turn into a Stockholm Syndrome love story."

I roll my eyes. "Yeah, right. More like a cautionary tale."

"Come on, spill! Was he like one of those tall, dark, and handsome mysteries we fantasize about in our book club?"

I let out a laugh. "Exactly. But he's so out of my league, it's not even funny." The thought of his commanding shoulders, firm chest, his towering form, and those comforting hands flood my mind. I jerk my head as if to physically cast away these thoughts.

Suddenly, my phone buzzes, jolting me. I glance at the screen; it's the insurance company calling.

"Great," I mutter under my breath, feeling a knot of anxiety. "It's about the bookstore."

Serena looks at me, worry etching her face. "Do you want me to stick around while you take that?"

I stand up, shaking my head. "No, I should handle this. Thanks, though, Ser. Really."

She gives me a quick hug and heads out. Just before the door shuts, Serena sends a playful air kiss my way.

"Love you," she whispers.

I catch it with a forced smile. "Love you too." I feel my anxiety creep up.

I close my eyes briefly, inhaling deeply, trying to calm the rapid breathing and the flutter in my chest. With a shaky hand, I finally tap "answer" on my phone, biting my lip nervously.

"Hello. Yes… yes… this is Laura Anne Thompson speaking."

The line crackles before a brisk, professional voice answers. "Good afternoon, Ms. Thompson. This is Rachel Green from First Assurance Insurance. I'm calling in regard to your claim for Thompson Tales of Fifth Ave."

My heart skips a beat. "Yes, about that…" I trail off, unsure what to expect.

Before heading off to Club V last night, I had already submitted the insurance claim online.

"Well, Ms. Thompson, we received an inquiry about a claim. However, we've noticed there have been no payments on your policy since March of last year."

I freeze.

*March?*

My mind races back. That's when David said he'd handle the insurance payments. My stomach churns. "You're saying… there have been no payments since then?"

"That's correct. We've sent multiple emails and physical letters to your address. The last was sent on June 15$^{th}$, and another on August 3rd addressed to Laura Anne Thompson. We've had no response."

I feel like throwing up.

*Emails, letters… all while I was drowning in book orders and trusting David.*

I bite my lip, tasting blood. "I… I never received them. I was scammed."

There's a pause on the line. "I'm very sorry, Ms. Thompson, but without the payments, your policy was terminated. We cannot cover your bookstore's damages."

*No, don't say it!*

My mind whirls. This can't be happening. I'm on the brink of losing everything.

"But… there must be something we can do?"

Rachel's voice is sympathetic but firm. "I'm afraid our hands are tied without an active policy, Ms. Thompson. I truly am sorry."

My throat tightens, a sense of dread washing over me. "Is there any way to reinstate it?

"To reinstate, you'd owe back payments plus a reinstatement fee. That's around fifty-eight thousand dollars. With the penalty, lawyer fees, and other charges, you're looking at a total of one hundred and twenty-eight thousand dollars." Rachel's voice is sympathetic but firm.

"One… one hundred and twenty-eight grand?" My voice cracks. "I can't… I don't have that kind of money."

Rachel's tone is cautious, almost hesitant. "Yes, Ms. Thompson, but even if you reinstate the policy, we can't cover the fire damage. It happened when your coverage was terminated."

A lump forms in my throat, choking off my words.

Her voice has a tinge of sympathy, but it's the kind that doesn't change a damn thing. "I'm really sorry, Ms. Thompson. This is a tough situation."

Tears blur my vision, unshed and burning.

"So, I lose my store, and there's nothing I can do?" I murmur.

"Ms. Thompson. I wish there was more we could do. If you need any assistance or have further questions, please don't hesitate to contact us." Her words, meant to be comforting, feel like salt in an open wound.

I hang up, my back sliding down the wall as I sit on the floor.

*I'm to blame.*

*That's it.*

*Game over.*

# Chapter 15

*Victor*

**I STRIDE** into the main house; the place reeks of luxury and old money. But, as always, it's as tense as a coiled spring. My father hates an audience. He keeps his circle tight, only a handful of soldiers he trusts. The rest is just sprawling land and this goddamn mansion.

Ksenia's holed up in her office, a command center that mirrors the severity of our world. Stark, functional, with the kind of affluence that speaks more of power than comfort. A large, imposing table anchors the room, a chandelier overhead casting stark shadows across the walls.

She's surrounded by a mountain of paperwork, the logistical brain behind our operations. Her mind is like a steel trap, especially when it comes to finances. She can sniff out discrepancies in the books faster than a hound.

"Building a paper fortress, Ksenia?" I jest as I enter.

Without missing a beat, she retorts, "Trying to keep the empire afloat. What do you want?"

I lean casually against the wall, observing her dissect the financial chaos. "Just checking in. How's the balance sheet looking?"

Ksenia glances up, her gaze sharp. "We're bleeding funds, Victor. You should pay more attention; that fifteen million dollars in cargo can't just disappear. We need to handle this."

"*Suka!*" A deep curse rumbles in my throat. "Misha and I are on it. Ivan's got to sit on it before they can repack the stuff and move it. Can't risk it getting sniffed out."

Ksenia's response is noncommittal, her gaze fixed on some point beyond the paperwork.

I probe further, "You still got a thing for Ivan Vasiliev?"

"Don't be an idiot, little brother," she snaps, shooting me a withering glare before turning her attention back to the mountain of paperwork. "Just keep your jokes to yourself. I'm not in the mood."

"Just double-checking—" Suddenly, I go silent, a faint noise catching my ear. It's barely there, but in our world, even the slightest sound can mean trouble.

Ksenia's expression instantly shifts to one of ice-cold alertness.

I tread quietly toward the bookshelf, every sense on edge, ready for anything. In a swift move, I pull back a book, yelling, "Gotcha!"

"Ahhhhhh!!" The high-pitched scream of a little girl pierces the tension, quickly dissolving into giggles.

"*Dyadya* Victor, you scared me!" Elizaveta exclaims, her beautiful gray eyes wide—the same eyes that Ksenia and I share.

I can't help but chuckle at her shock. "Sneaking around isn't safe, Eli. You shouldn't be listening in on grown-up talk."

She smirks, a spark of mischief in her eyes. "But I did so well! Mommy and you didn't even know I was here for so long!"

Seeing her so proud, I can't resist giving her a big hug, lifting her off the ground. I plant a kiss on her cheek, feeling a surge of affection for this bright spark in our often-grim world.

"You're too clever for your own good, kiddo."

Eli giggles, wrapping her small arms around my neck. "I want to be smart like Mommy and strong like you, *Dyadya* Victor."

I set her down on a chair, ruffling her hair. "You're already on your way, trust me. But remember, being smart means knowing when to keep out of trouble."

"*Dyadya* Victor, who is Ivan Vasi… Vasiliev?" she stumbles over the name, trying to get her tongue around the unfamiliar sounds. "Is he a bad guy, *Dyadya* Victor?

*Shit. She heard everything.* I shoot a side-eye at Ksenia.

"Well, he's our enemy!" Ksenia declares matter-of-factly.

Elizaveta's eyes widen, forming an "O" shape with her mouth. "Did our enemy steal from us?"

"No, Mommy and I were just joking, Eli," I quickly say, trying to shield her from the harsher truths of our world.

"Yes, he did," my sister interjects, her voice firm.

I spin around to face Ksenia, frustration clear on my face.

*What the hell is she doing, exposing Eli to all this?*

Quickly tuning into my silent plea for discretion, Ksenia dismisses it with a wave of her hand. "Eli's more aware than you think. We don't sugarcoat truths in this house,"

*Blyad! She's just eight years old, for crying out loud.*

A knot of discomfort twists in my gut.

It's hard, too damn hard, seeing Eli, this little beacon of innocence, getting a crash course in our brutal reality.

"Hey, Eli, where's Yuri?" I ask, trying to steer her young mind away from our grim business. I watch her face light up at the mention of her older brother.

Ksenia is already on her phone, her tone curt. "Nina, come pick up Ms. Elizaveta from my office." There's a hint of annoyance in her voice. She's gone through a string of nannies—no surprise, considering Eli's a whirlwind of energy, always one step ahead.

"Yuri is with Papa. They have *biz-ness*," Eli pronounces the word carefully, her young voice trying to mimic our seriousness.

My heart sinks a bit. *"Business with Papa"* means Yuri, at just eighteen, is already entangled in the Bratva life.

Quiet, serious Yuri, so much like Ksenia—sharp as a tack with numbers, already neck-deep in some of our more complicated dealings. A smart kid, but I can't help feeling a pang of regret that he's being pulled into this life so young.

Just then, Nina, the latest in a long line of nannies, rushes into the office. Her face is etched with fear, a clear sign that handling Eli is more than just a regular babysitting gig.

"Forgive me, Madam Ksenia," she falters, anxiety etched on her face. "Ms. Elizaveta, we must go now." Her voice shakes with evident fear.

Elizaveta, undeterred by the nanny's clear anxiety, hops down from her chair with the same bright energy. "Bye, *Dyadya* Victor! Bye, Mommy!"

After I plant a kiss on Eli's pink cheeks and watch her scamper away with Nina, I make sure the door is securely shut. Turning back to Ksenia, my anger simmers to the surface.

"*Ksusha*, this is fucked up. Eli's just a kid, she shouldn't be anywhere near this shit. And Yuri? He's barely more than a kid himself," I growl, my frustration obvious.

Ksenia's face is set in stone as she meets my gaze. "They're Morozovs, Victor. Better they learn what that means now rather than later," she replies coldly.

I shake my head, disgusted. This is exactly why I am not interested in having children. Bringing a new life into this twisted world, only to see it corrupted?

*Hell no.* I won't let my own blood be tainted by this life.

"You've always been the sentimental one, Victor," Ksenia remarks, a hint of disdain in her voice. "You're going to be a husband and a father soon, leading this Bratva as a *Pakhan*."

"I'm not sentimental, Ksenia," I snap back defensively.

"You are. Haven't forgotten you crying under the blanket for months when Mama died," she throws at me, her words sharp as knives.

"I was *nine*, for fuck's sake!" I retort, the memory stinging like a fresh wound.

"Morozovs don't cry, Victor." She stares piercingly into my eyes. "Even if we're being skinned alive."

"*Blyad*, I'll rest in my grave, not before!" my father's voice thunders.

I step into the opulent room, the air thick with tension. This isn't just any bedroom; it's a command center, draped in luxury, a testament to the Morozov legacy. And there, in the eye of the storm, is the *Pakhan* himself, my father, Andrey Morozov.

He's propped up like a king in exile, all wiry muscle and barely restrained rage. The very picture of a caged beast. Our family doctor, Dr. Petrov—a man as tough as they come, who's seen more bullet wounds than natural illnesses—stands at the bedside, facing off with the old man.

"*Vy dolzhny proyti operatsiyu*, Andrey." His voice is steady, but the *Pakhan's* having none of it.

My father's laugh is a harsh bark. "Operation? I'll go under the knife when I'm dead, Petrov. Not a moment sooner."

Dr. Petrov doesn't back down. "Andrey, keep pushing, and you'll find yourself in a grave. You think you're tough? Death doesn't discriminate. You had a stroke, not a scratch. Act like it."

"I built this empire on blood and iron, not by cowering under sheets," my father retorts.

The doctor's stance remains firm, like a rock against the tide. "This isn't about fear; it's about sense. You're playing a fool's game, challenging death like this."

The air is thick with the clash of two titanic wills.

Petrov, a man who's stared down the worst, isn't about to be cowed by even the *Pakhan's* fury. He is no ordinary doctor; this is a man who's been part of our lives, part of the Bratva's fabric since I was just a kid.

He runs his hands over his thick gray hair. With his rugged handsomeness and eyes that carry a hint of sadness, he is a figure who commands respect. In his late fifties, he is still well-built, a reminder of his days within the Bratva before he chose the path of healing over bloodshed. You can tell from one look that this man isn't someone to be taken lightly. His presence in a room is as commanding as any seasoned soldier.

I remember him, even from when I was just a boy—always there, a constant in the turbulent sea of our lives. He'd stitch us up, set broken bones, never once flinching at the brutal reality of our world. But it was more than that. Petrov chose to be a healer in a world where violence was the language. He's seen the worst we have to offer, yet he chose to save lives rather than take them.

Now, as he stands before the *Pakhan*, there's a heavy tension. It's the kind of respect born from years in the trenches together, yet now on opposing sides of this particular battle.

*For fuck's sake.*

I clear my throat, stepping closer. "Papa, the doctor's right. We need you in command, not courting death over pride."

My father's eyes, fierce as ever, turn to me. "Victor, you worry about the Bratva. I'll worry about me."

Petrov's gaze doesn't waver. "Victor's right, Andrey. Your pride might just kill you before your enemies do."

"My enemies will tear apart everything I've built if they see any weakness," he grunts. He tries to stand, a futile show of strength that falls flat. His body rebels and it's like watching a king lose his crown.

*Blyad.*

It hurts somewhere deep inside me, but I'm not about to let it show.

"Then let them see strength through me," I counter, my voice hard. "As long as I'm here, the Bratva is secure. But if you don't go through with this operation…"

My father's eyes narrow, assessing. "I'm not stepping back until you're at the helm, Victor. Married, settled. The *Pakhan* needs an heir, not just a title."

My jaw tightens. This old-school thinking, it's a noose around our necks.

"Fine. If that's what it takes," I shoot back, my voice cold. "But the bride will be my choice. No debates. And heir talk can wait. I'll deal with it when I'm damn well ready."

A grudging respect flickers in my father's eyes. "Always fucking hard-headed, aren't you? Fine, choose your bride. But she must be strong enough to stand beside the Morozov name."

"Don't worry about the Morozov name, Papa. Just focus on not kicking the bucket too soon. I've got the bride part covered," I shoot back with a wry grin.

Petrov shakes his head. "You two are cut from the same stubborn cloth."

"He's my son, after all. Did you expect any less?" my father retorts with a faint smirk, his tone a blend of pride and challenge. "When I was your age, I was already married with you kids, leading legions in the Bratva," he boasts, his voice tinged with pride. "You've got big shoes to fill, Victor. Let's see how you measure up."

I roll my eyes at my father's backhanded compliment.

In his world, words are weapons, not tools for encouragement. It's always about being tougher, stronger, more feared.

"You know, Papa, while you're busy reminiscing, I've been expanding the Bratva's reach," I say, leaning against the doorframe. "We're not just thugs on the street anymore. We've got construction projects, hotels, housing—a whole damn empire under our belt."

He gives me a skeptical look, as if challenging me to prove my worth. "Expanding, huh? Just don't forget, son, it's not just about building empires. It's about holding onto them."

"Trust me, I haven't forgotten. You think those territories were handed to us on a silver platter? It took some... persuasive methods to secure them."

My father's lips twitch in a semblance of a smile, but his eyes are hard. "Just don't lose sight of what's important. This family, our name—that's your first priority."

I can feel my patience wearing thin. "I know what's at stake, Papa. I'm not some green kid anymore." He's about to retort, but I cut him off. "Yeah, Papa, history lessons some other time. Right now, just don't give Petrov a heart attack, okay?"

Winking at Petrov, I say, "He's all yours now. Good luck," and quickly exit the room.

Stepping into the hallway, I exhale deeply, a mix of worry and frustration for my father weighing on me.

*Don't be a pussy, Victor.*

Vulnerability doesn't have a place in our home.

It takes me back to when Mama died. Ksenia and I... we weren't allowed to cry, not even as we watched her life slip away in that sudden, brutal car crash. It was swift, they said, as if that lessened the agony.

Papa stood there, his face an impenetrable mask, expecting us to be as unyielding. Tears were for the weak, and Morozovs were never weak. Even as a kid, I knew better than to let my guard down. That moment... it changed us, hardened us. In the Morozov household, grief, fear, pain—they were to be locked away, out of sight.

Now, facing the reality of my father's frailty, those old, unyielding rules still hold.

No cracks in the armor, not now, not ever.

I smash the "call" button, and he's there like a shot.

"Misha, there's something I need done," I tell him. "Gather a team; someone needs a little… persuasion."

# Chapter 16

*Laura*

***NOW, WHAT*** *the hell am I supposed to do?*

*I'm royally screwed.*

I stand up and pace around my apartment like a caged animal, the walls closing in on me. Every nook and cranny feels tainted with memories of David.

My mind is a whirlwind, thoughts colliding and spiraling out of control.

I want to scream, to release this pent-up anger.

The thought of strangling David, watching the shock in his eyes, is both terrifying and satisfying. I hate that he's reduced me to this—to violent fantasies and bitter resentment.

"Rot in hell!"

My feet carry me to a corner that I've ignored for too long, a space filled with his belongings that I never dared to touch.

*Screw you!*

Frustrated, I start rummaging through his stuff, things I've avoided touching since he left.

I open drawers, flip through papers, searching for... something. Anything that could give me a clue to the question: *Why me?*

I dig deeper until my hands find a folder tucked away, hidden under a pile of his old sweatshirts. My fingers tremble as I pull it out. The folder is thick, bulging with papers, and as I flip it open, my heart drops.

*Jesus.*

They're letters, unopened, addressed to me, from the insurance company. My breath catches in my throat as I tear through them, one after the other. Notices of missed payments, warnings, final reminders.

Like a hammer blow to my gut. David had been hiding these from me all along.

The bastard planned it all—to screw me over, swipe my savings, let the shop's insurance slide into oblivion.

*Laur, you've been duped big time. But why?*

My hands clench into fists, the paper crinkling under my grip. I want to scream, to let out this storm brewing inside me.

I tear through the damn letters, my hands shaking with a fury I can barely contain. "Fuck this!" I yell into the silence of my cramped apartment.

I thought I knew David, but he's been playing me all along. I remember the first time he walked into Thompson Tales, that innocent look in his eyes.

*How could someone so seemingly sweet screw me over like this?*

"You son of a bitch," I mutter, venom lacing my voice. I lash out at the pile of his things shoved into the corner—a mess of boxes he had told me never to touch. A black case skids across the floor, opening with a clatter, revealing its hollow insides—an empty gun case.

"Jesus Christ…" A sharp breath escapes me, my mind racing. "What the hell was he mixed up in?"

I slump against the wall. Eyes wide open.

*Who the fuck did I marry?*

All those late nights he came home, claiming he was entertaining clients.

*What clients? What was he really doing?*

My mind's a whirlwind of questions with no damn answers. Every late night, every mysterious phone call—it all adds up to a picture I don't want to see.

*How could I have been so blind?*

The taste of iron floods my mouth as I bite down on my lip. "What did you get me into, David?" I whisper to the empty room.

I need answers, and I need them now. I stand up, the urge to tear through every corner of this place overwhelming me. I start with his desk, pulling open drawers with reckless abandon, papers and pens flying. Nothing but old receipts and useless junk.

I move to his closet, yanking clothes off hangers, tossing shoes aside. Then, buried at the back, I find it—a briefcase I've never seen before. My hands tremble as I work the clasps, the metallic clicks far too loud in the silence of the room. The case opens with a sigh, revealing its contents. Inside, there are more papers, documents with names and numbers that make no sense.

Among the sea of papers, something catches my eye. "Is... that a diary?" I whisper to myself. Its cover is a deep color of old blood.

Picking it up, it feels like a relic in my hands, with edges that look like it's worn from years of clandestine handling. I crack it open, the spine creaking with the sound of secrets long buried. The musty scent of old paper and ink hits me, the kind of smell that tells stories of backroom deals and hushed conversations.

"It's... a ledger." My hands tremble as I sift through the papers. My eyes strain to decipher the scrawled handwriting, names and figures dancing before me in an indecipherable waltz of crime and currency.

It's a *ledger*, alright, but not for some mom-and-pop store—this is a meticulous record of illicit transactions.

"Vasiliev Corp... What the hell?" I mutter to myself. The entries are dizzying in their scope: accounts of smuggled contraband and lists of bribes paid out to silhouetted figures with code names. There are amounts that could buy small countries, all casually noted next to dates and cryptic references.

It's David's handwriting that stands out in the newer entries, unmistakable and bold. I trace the lines with a trembling finger, each word a nail in the coffin of the life I thought I knew.

He's been cataloging everything—kilos of drugs, payoffs, and dirty money that's flowed through this mysterious Vasiliev Corp.

My breath hitches in my throat as I stare at the ledger, its contents a barrage of criminal shorthand.

"Ivan... Ivan...?" I attempt, the name feeling alien. "Vasi..liev ?" I'm butchering the pronunciation, but there's no one to correct me, just the silent accusation of ink on paper.

"*Klinika*... Some clinic thing," I murmur, noticing a bunch of clinics getting weirdly big deliveries. Then there are these names, big shots in the government, scribbled next to crazy amounts of cash. "Half a million," I whisper, "for what? Keeping quiet? Playing along?"

"Oh, my God." Suddenly, it all clicks.

The pages are a catalog of corruption, and David's meticulous entries grow clearer, his neat script cataloging each transaction. "Transport completion," one entry reads, followed by a sum that could buy silence or worse.

There's a note: "Assassination completion—one hundred and twenty thousand," and a name that could headline any newspaper.

"Fuck me," I breathe out, the reality hitting me hard. David wasn't just hiding letters. He was hiding a whole other life.

I close the ledger with a snap, sinking back onto the floor, the briefcase splayed open in front of me. The reality of David's world is hitting hard on me. This was no regular accounting book; it was a ledger of secrets and sins. The kind of book that could get a person killed.

"Is this who you really were all along?" I whisper, my hands trembling as I clutch the ledger.

*What do I do with this? Go to the cops?*

The realization that I'm holding possibly incriminating evidence makes me want to drop it as if it were on fire.

I pry up the loose floorboard I discovered by accident last summer and never fixed—a perfect hiding spot. The ledger slides in, just fitting into this secret compartment. I replace the board and drag the small side table over it, a makeshift seal over a Pandora's box of troubles.

*Should I tell Serena? No, this feels too dangerous.*

*Now what?* The question circles in my head like a vulture. I can't just sit here.

I start pacing, my gaze darting around the room, landing on the slightly ajar window.

A shiver rolls down between my shoulder blades. I don't remember opening it. I shuffle across the room and slam the window shut. Curtains drawn, I turn back to the room, a fortress against prying eyes.

Then, the sound of my phone vibrating on my table shatters the quiet apartment.

"Jesus!" My heart leaps into my throat. I march over to the table, my pulse racing. The phone's screen flashes an unknown number. Warily, I hit "answer," pressing the phone to my ear.

"Hello?" My voice is a whisper, tension winding tight in my chest.

Silence greets me, just the distant noise of traffic. It's creepy, like someone's watching, waiting.

"Hello? Who is this?" I'm getting annoyed now, my voice rising.

Still nothing. It's like they're playing some sick game.

"Why are you calling?" I snap, louder. "What do you want?"

Then, just like that, they hang up. The line goes dead. I stare at the phone, a knot of fear in my gut.

*Who the hell was that?*

With the phone still in my hand, it vibrates with an incoming call. Annoyed and on edge, I answer without even glancing at the caller ID. "Look, you freak, if you think scaring me is…" My voice trails off as I recognize the voice on the other end. It's Mr. Henderson, my landlord.

"M-Mr. Henderson?" My face heats up with embarrassment. "I'm sorry, I didn't mean to—" I start, but he interrupts.

"I've seen your shop, Laura. It's a disaster. What's happening? Have you filed the insurance claim?" His voice is stern, demanding.

I wince, rubbing my temple. "Mr. Henderson, I... I need more time. There's been a complication." The words feel heavy, laden with unspoken truths about David's betrayal.

He coughs, a deep, rattling sound. "I'll be in town tomorrow. We need to talk. Face to face." The line goes dead before I can respond.

I stare at the phone, the weight of the situation pressing down on me. Then, the unknown number flashes again.

"Hello?" I answer, exasperation bleeding into my tone.

A pause, then a familiar voice sends a shiver down my spine. "Run."

"Da-David?"

Before I have a chance to process the call, a chilling sensation creeps over me. A shadow stretches across the floor, growing larger, inching closer.

*Holy hell, who's that?*

I turn, but it's too late.

A large hand, swift and sure, clamps down over my mouth, silencing the scream that's building in my throat.

# Chapter 17

*Laura*

"MOMMY?"

I'm standing in our old living room, watching my mother as she sits at her writing desk. Her face is younger, her pen moves frantically across the paper, her expression a blend of intense focus and pure happiness.

"Laura honey, come here," she calls, a smile lighting up her face, her eyes sparkling with the thrill of creation.

I get closer, curious. "What's this story about, Mommy?" my younger voice asks simply, watching her write.

"It's about a little girl who dreams big," she answers, her voice brimming with excitement. "She travels through wondrous lands, meets magical creatures, and faces challenges with bravery and heart."

"The little girl, does she find what she's looking for?" I ask, completely drawn in.

"Every step is a discovery," she says. "She learns about courage, friendship, and the magic within herself. It's a journey of wonder and daring, a story to remind us all to dream and explore."

"I wanna have adventures, too, Mommy," I say with a smile, touching her cheek. "I miss you so much."

She kisses my cheek gently. "Silly girl, I'm right here with you."

Then, the moment shatters. "Don't be ridiculous!" my father's voice cuts through, dripping with scorn. "Your stories are pointless. No one cares about them."

I want to stand up for Mommy, to scream at him to leave her alone.

But I can't. I just watch as Mommy's face falls, her light dimming.

Soon, she stops writing. The table, once cluttered with papers and pens, now hosts a collection of empty bottles, her bed becoming her world. I try to write with her, to bring back the spark, but she can't—or won't—get up.

"Mommy, no…"

The room fades into darkness.

There's my mother again, but this time, she's different—haggard, her eyes dull. More of those empty bottles clutter the table where her stories once blossomed.

"Mommy, please, let me help you," I plead, extending my hand toward her. "Let's get rid of all this pain and start over together." Wanting to wipe away the pain, the addiction, the slow destruction.

"Mommy?" I reach out to touch her. Her head lolls back grotesquely, eyes rolling up, blood trickling from the corner of her mouth. "No, no, no, Mommy! Please..." My cries echo in the void, tears streaming down my face.

"Stupid woman." My father's shadow looms over us, his voice cruel. "Serves her right." His laughter is a harsh, grating sound.

"No!" I scream at him. "Go away!" I want him to disappear, but his laughter only grows, a booming mockery in the darkness.

I snap my eyes open, my heart racing, cold sweat coating my skin. It's that same haunting dream that's been chasing me since I was eighteen, the day I discovered Mom lying lifeless in her bed.

Brushing the tears from my face, I let out a shaky breath.

The dream's grip loosens, but the room's reality hits hard. Lifting my head, I'm awed by the ceiling. It's huge, ridiculously high, dwarfing me beneath its vast expanse of elaborate plasterwork.

*This isn't my place.*

The bed beneath me is too soft, the sheets too silky.

*Where am I?*

I sit up slowly, my head spinning, trying to piece together the fragments of memory from the night before, but before I can even start to figure things out, I am taken aback by the room.

Blinking hard, my eyes take in the scene. This room... it's like nothing I've ever seen. It's like stepping into a fairy tale—all pastel pinks and soft, luxurious fabrics. The delicate glow from the crystal chandelier above casts a warm light over everything, highlighting the opulence of the furnishings.

*What the actual hell?*

I spot the door across the room, half expecting someone to burst in any second. But the door stays firmly closed. Surreal. Clutching the bedsheet, my mind racing, the memory of what happened crashes over me like a wave.

*The ledger, David, and the break-in at my apartment, the shadowy figure, and then... darkness.*

*Oh, God.* Fear prickles over my nerve endings as I realize the gravity of my situation.

I'm not just in a strange room; *I'm a captive.*

Slipping my toes off the bed carefully, I feel the plush rug under my feet. "Wha-what? This rug is probably worth a fortune," I whisper, a bit overwhelmed.

*Is this a dream?*

Pinching myself, I flinch. "Ouch! Nope, definitely not dreaming." A chill breeze from the window cracked open. Weirdly quiet in here, like too quiet.

*What's this twisted game?*

My eyes widen as I take in the bizarre scene—toys scattered around, children's books stacked in a neat pile; my attention shifts to the picture frames lining the walls. Each one features the same little girl, a bright smile on her face, gray eyes sparkling with mischief, and dark hair cascading in gentle waves.

There's something hauntingly familiar about those eyes, like I've seen them before... *but where*?

I stand up, my movements cautious, and as I walk past a giant mirror, I freeze.

*What the...?*

Glancing down at myself, I see the cashmere robe clinging softly to my figure. It's elegant, way too elegant for a simple sleeping outfit. The fabric is smooth against my skin, a rich cream color that contrasts sharply with my bewildered expression in the mirror. It's like I'm dressed for a fancy sleepover, not like someone who's been kidnapped.

*Are you kidding me right now?*

"Who changed my clothes?" I whisper to myself. And who strips a kidnapped woman and dresses her in luxury nightwear?

Out of nowhere, I catch a glimpse of movement in the mirror, a small figure appearing behind me. For a moment, I think I'm seeing things.

"Ahhh!" I can't help but let out a startled yelp. I spin around so fast I almost trip.

Standing right behind me is the girl from the picture frames, real as day. My heart's doing a crazy dance, and for a split second, I'm half-convinced I'm about to wet myself.

"What? Who are you?" I blurt out, my heart pounding. "Are you a ghost?" As soon as I say it, I realize how ridiculous it sounds.

*Great, Laura, talking to ghosts now, are we?*

The girl laughs, her eyes twinkling with mischief. "Yes... Boo!" she teases, taking a step closer.

Her eyes dancing with mischief. "Gotcha!"

I squint at her, almost certain I've lost it. "So, you're actually real, huh? Didn't just pop out of a picture frame or something, right?" I mumble, unsure if I'm hoping for a yes or a no.

She rolls her eyes dramatically. "Of course, I'm real!" She comes closer. "I'm Elizaveta, but you can call me Eli. And you're in my room!"

"Well, Eli, you nearly gave me a heart attack." I can't help but chuckle despite the surrealness of the situation.

She grins, proud of her little stunt. "You should've seen your face! It was like this!" She scrunches up her face in a comical expression of terror.

"Wait. I'm in your room?" I glance around again, finally connecting the dots—the toys, the books, it's all stuff that would belong to a kid.

"Yes, I beg Mommy to have a sleepover in my room." Eli beams, her smile infectious. Despite the bizarreness of my situation, her cheerfulness is hard to resist. It's like she's a tiny beacon of light in this confusing darkness.

*A sleepover?*

*Who is "Mommy"?*

"Eli, do you know… who brought me here?" My voice falters, a mix of confusion and a creeping sense of dread.

*How do you even ask a kid why you've been kidnapped?*

Eli just shrugs nonchalantly, twirling a lock of her hair around her finger. "Don't know," she chirps. Her casualness about the whole thing is almost comical. "Mommy says you're going to marry *Dyadya* Vi…"

"Eli, that's enough." The sharp command makes both of us spin around.

"Mommy!" Eli exclaims, rushing to the woman and wrapping her arms around her legs. "She's funny," she whispers loudly, casting a glance back at me.

My eyes follow Eli's scamper to the commanding figure in the doorway. Standing in the doorway is a woman with an air of authority that's almost tangible. She's striking. *Holy moly.* She might just be the most stunning woman I've ever laid eyes on.

Her dress clings to her like a second skin, a deep black that contrasts sharply with the whimsical decor of the room. The fabric hugs every curve of her hourglass figure, and the slit along the thigh suggests a blend of sophistication and peril. Her hair, dark as the dress, flows in voluminous waves, framing a face that could grace any magazine cover.

*Holy smokes, she's drop-dead gorgeous and absolutely terrifying.*

Her eyes get me, gray and sharp as shards of ice. They pin me down, all the power and mystery in the world crammed into those irises. She walks in, and it's like the dark corners of the room get the memo to back off. The light bends around her like she's the boss of it.

And those eyes... *Where have I seen those eyes before?*

They soften momentarily as she looks down at Eli. "I see you've made our guest feel at home in your room," she says, her voice laced with a hint of amusement.

"Hello," I start, my voice low and husky. "But I think there's been some mistake..." I clear my throat, trying to find my voice.

She fixes her gaze on me, her eyes scrutinizing yet unreadable. "Ksenia," she introduces herself crisply, her voice carrying a hint of an accent. "There's no mistake, Laura."

*She knows my name?*

Eli's grip tightens around her. "Mommy says you're gonna be family, so you're in my room! I wanted you to feel at home," she says, her eyes shining with excitement.

*What?*

Eli tugs at Ksenia's dress, bringing her down to whisper range. "Mommy," she stage-whispers, not quite the secret she thinks it is, "she's going to be the most beautiful bride."

*Huh?* Guess this must be some mistaken identity mix-up.

Ksenia's gaze doesn't waver from me, but a small smile tugs at the corner of her mouth. "Is that so?" Her tone is light, but I sense something sharp hiding behind her words.

I feel like I'm missing pieces of a puzzle, the whole picture frustratingly out of reach.

*Who?*

*Me?*

*Bride?*

# Chapter 18

*Laura*

"I... I don't understand." I cough out a dry, panicky laugh. "You're a real prankster, Eli," I manage to say.

I glance back and forth between her and Ksenia. "I'm not anyone's... *bride*."

"Eli, I think it's time for you to go get your *Dyadya*," Ksenia instructs smoothly, her eyes never leaving mine. "He must be glad that his new bride is awake."

*Run.*

But my legs are rooted to the spot, as if the plush rug has turned to quicksand.

"Okay, Mommy!" Eli skips out of the room, leaving me alone with Ksenia.

The room falls into a heavy silence.

*Hit her, Laura, then run fast.*

Yet, I stand frozen, mesmerized by the intimidating woman before me.

"Look, I'm up to my neck in trouble," I spit out, the words tumbling in a rush. "I've got a bookstore that's nothing but ashes now and no insurance to cover anything. I can't be caught up in whatever madness this is."

A smile plays on Ksenia's lips, but her eyes remain as cold as steel.

*Note to self: sob stories don't work on stone-cold kidnappers. My life drama is just white noise to her.*

"Come in," she commands, gesturing to someone outside the door.

The door opens, and two men step in—tall, broad-shouldered, dressed in impeccably tailored black suits. They look like they've walked straight out of a mobster movie.

"Wait, what's happening?" I stammer, my eyes darting between Ksenia and the men.

Ksenia doesn't answer. Instead, she watches, almost detached, as the men approach me.

"Hey, wait a minute!" I blurt out as they close in. "You're making a mistake!" I attempt a quick escape, but they catch me easily, their hands clamping down on my arms like vises. "Let go, you jerks!" I squirm and twist, trying to break free, but they're like human walls, immovable and unyielding.

"You've got the wrong person!" I protest. I try to twist away, but it's like fighting against a wall.

"Wait just a second! You can't do this, you... you gloriously terrifying goddess of doom! I know who you are now, *Ksenia*! And let me tell you, there's a special place in hell for stunningly beautiful kidnappers! This is some serious law-breaking stuff, and trust me, it won't end well for you. My army of angry friends, not to mention the police, are probably storming the gates as we speak!" I try to catch Ksenia's attention, but her expression remains unreadable, her eyes cold and calculating.

The men yank me out of the room, and I sneak a last glance at Ksenia. She's just sighing and shaking her head like she's disappointed or *something.*

*What was that?*

As soon as we leave Eli's room, the house unfolds before me. It's like a scene from a gothic movie—luxurious, opulent, and eerily silent.

My mind races, fear mingling with a sense of awe. "Where are you taking me?" I ask, my voice trembling. One of the men just gives me a brief, emotionless glance, his grip unyielding like iron shackles.

*Oh, Jesus.*

*Hollyfuckingshit.*

My feet drag against the plush carpet as they lead me down the ostentatious corridor. The lavish decor does little to distract me from the dread building in my stomach.

I throw out another feeble threat, my voice weaker now. "You can't do this. People will be looking for me!"

They don't say a word, just carry me down the stairs like I'm some kind of mannequin.

By now, my steps become more resigned. The cold marble beneath my feet is a stark contrast to the warmth of Eli's room; the statues and paintings that adorn the hallways seem to watch me with silent judgment.

Reaching the bottom, I catch sight of a heavy, ornate door. It looks more like the entrance to a fortress than a room.

"Let go... of... me!" I shout, but the sound fades, useless. They're immovable, holding me firm as we near the door. I've stopped struggling now, the futility of my efforts sinking in. My body feels heavy, every step dragging more than the last.

One of the men knocks on the door, his voice gruff but respectful. "Boss, she's here."

As the door swings open, one of the men shoves me forward so abruptly I almost face-plant into the plush rug. "Hey!" I protest, my indignation flaring up. "Ever heard of manners, you Neanderthal?"

"He's waiting for you," grunts one of the suits as they lock me in.

The door shuts with a definitive click.

*Fuck!*

"Who's waiting for me? You lunatics!" My voice cracks as I pound on the sturdy wood, the thuds of my fists futile against its mass. "Let me out of here!"

Silence.

"Alright, off to find the mystery man," I holler, my words bouncing off the walls and back to me.

Pointless.

And there it is: my white flag moment.

I spin on my heel, heart pounding like a runaway train in my chest, and— *Whoa. What?* My mouth hangs open, any lingering anger zapped away for a second as my eyes take in the scene before me—a room that feels like a step back in time. The walls are lined with shelves brimming with books, their spines a kaleidoscope of faded colors and gold lettering.

I smell the musky scent of old paper and leather, mixed with a hint of cigar smoke lingering in the background.

*Mmm, that old book scent is amazing.*

*Snap out of it! Laura, remember, you've been kidnapped!*

My bare feet sink into the rug, like stepping on a cloud—way too fancy for a kidnapping scene if you ask me. The room is lined with shelves of books from floor to ceiling. Some are old, their spines cracked and worn, while others look newer. A large desk sits at the far end, more like a centerpiece than a piece of furniture.

I feel a weird mix of awe and panic. It's like stepping into someone's private world, a place where important decisions are made. The silence is thick, only broken by the soft sound of my own breathing.

Taking cautious steps, I look around. "Hello?" I whisper to myself.

I pause.

Glancing over my shoulder, I half-expect some lurking figure to leap out at me. With a cautious breath, I take a few more steps. I can't help but read the book titles on the shelves.

Then my eyes land on a book with the title "The Histories by Herodotus." I pull it out from the shelf, my hands shaking as I realize what I'm holding. "No way! A first edition?" I whisper, awe-struck. This isn't just some old book; it's a piece of history, probably worth more than my entire apartment.

"This is insane," I murmur, carefully running my fingers over the ancient pages.

Immediately next to where the book was, I spot "Lost Chronicles of Alexander the Great," and my heart leaps. "You've got to be kidding me," I say, pulling it out gingerly. The weight of it in my hands feels like holding a treasure.

"This is the kind of book collectors would sell their souls for." My voice is hushed, reverent, as I realize the rarity of what I'm touching.

I glance around the room, still clutching the books.

*Fuck me!* This room is a book nerd's paradise, and I'm trapped in it.

"Of all the places to end up," I chuckle nervously, "a billionaire's personal library isn't the worst." I feel a mix of terror and exhilaration.

*Great! I can still crack a joke mid-meltdown.*

Carefully, I place the books back, my fingers lingering on the spine. "I can't believe I'm seeing this with my own eyes." My heart's still racing, not just from fear but from the thrill of being surrounded by such priceless artifacts.

"This room must be worth a fortune," I whisper to myself, a sense of disbelief washing over me.

Taking a deep breath, I try to calm my racing heart.

*Okay, Laura, focus. You're in a kidnapper's den, not a book fair.*

CLING.

Startled by the sudden click in the eerie quiet, I jerk back. My heart's pounding loud enough to drown out the silence.

"What the—?" slips out before I can stop it. I slap a hand over my mouth, biting back a shout.

Then, that unmistakable whiff of cigar smoke hits me. Someone's here, smoking a cigar in this room! Panic flickers through me.

*What if it starts a fire…?*

Then, driven by a mix of fear and curiosity, my feet begin moving almost on their own.

I find myself at the far end of the room, standing before a grand table and a chair that screams royalty, more throne than seat.

Sunlight seeps through heavy velvet drapes, casting a dramatic, almost cinematic glow. The kind you'd see in old Dracula movies.

"Who's there?" My voice is just a whisper, lost in the grandeur of the room. There's a slight movement from the chair, a subtle shift.

The next moment, a flicker of light from a cigar briefly reveals a face hidden in shadows. My eyes lock onto his—those same piercing gray eyes I've seen before.

I gasp, frozen in place.

*No freaking way.*

Then, breaking the tense silence, a voice—deep, familiar, and unnervingly calm—speaks.

"Hello, little firecracker," Victor Morozov greets me with a smirk. "You didn't listen, did you? I told you to wait for me at the hotel, but you just had to defy me."

# Chapter 19

*Victor*

**GOVNO.**

She drives me mad.

The sunlight blasting in from behind me turns her nightgown into a damn X-ray, showcasing every curve. Her skin glows against that stark white, making it hard to focus on anything else.

*Fucking great.*

Because she's got my cock twitching and throbbing with a mind of its own.

Fucking her on this vintage table is all I can think about. I imagine grabbing her roughly and throwing her onto the table, teasing and taunting her sweet pink cunt mercilessly and watching her squirming beneath me with need. And when she begs for my cock, I would give it to her hard and fast. Hear her crying out my name.

*Blyad! How has she got me all twisted up like this?*

"You?" She's in shock, her eyes wide as she takes in the room, the books, and then me.

"Yes. Me." I nod, watching the storm brewing in Laura's eyes.

*How, very interesting.*

Then, like a flash, she's up and at me. She leans across the desk, her face fucking gorgeous. Her eyes are blazing, the kind of fury you don't forget.

"What is *WRONG* with you?!" She's not just angry; she's nuclear.

I casually snuff out my cigar, but before I can even flick the ash, a book flies off the desk, heading straight for my face. Reflexes kick in; I catch it… barely.

*Shit, she's got a temper on her.*

"You. you think this is funny?" Her voice hits a snag, choked up in the middle—she's holding tears from streaming down her face.

*Fuck. She's beautiful when she's all kinds of mad.*

I raise an eyebrow. "Well… a little." Can't help my honesty.

Rage shakes her. "You kidnapped me! You… you…"

"Yep, that was me." Watching her, I'm fascinated by her meltdown. It's like witnessing a storm up close.

She bites her lip so hard I see red. Not a figure of speech; there's actual blood. Nervous habit or not, a rush of something I can't quite name courses through me.

Rising from my seat, I approach her, my movements deliberate and casting my shadow right over her.

She halts, eyes locked on mine. I can see panic rippling through her.

"Relax, hurting you isn't on my agenda, *kiska*." I state clearly.

Laura's worry makes sense, but she's exactly who I need for this.

Her shoulders drop a notch, easing up, but her eyes stay sharp, watching me like a hawk.

Fuck, I've never craved anything as intensely as I do now. My knuckles turn white from the pressure of my grip, desire pulsing through my veins like a fever.

"You're bleeding." I grab her chin gently yet firmly, making sure she's looking right at me. There's a moment, right before I kiss her, where I can practically hear her heart racing. And then I do—kiss her, I mean. It's soft, but there's a taste of blood. Her blood. And damn, if it doesn't light a fire in me.

She doesn't push me away.

Instead, there's this hesitation, like she's fighting with herself about how to feel.

It's a kiss that's supposed to show her I'm in charge, but the taste of her, that hint of blood, throws me off my game.

And then, just as I'm about to deepen the kiss, to really stake my claim, she fucking bites me. Hard.

I jerk back, more out of surprise than pain. My tongue darts out, tasting my own blood now.

Laura's eyes are wide, her chest heaving. She looks like she can't quite believe what she just did.

Neither can I.

A slow, wicked grin spreads across my face. "Well, well, *kotyonok*. Looks like this kitten has claws."

She glares at me, defiant even now. "I'm not your fucking kitten."

I laugh, deep and throaty. God, she's a feisty one. It only makes me want her more.

"We'll see about that," I murmur, stepping closer.

She backs up, but there's nowhere to go. I've got her cornered, trapped between me and the wall.

I lean in, my lips brushing her ear. "You know, I've always liked a challenge."

She shivers, and I can practically feel the goosebumps rising on her skin. "Fuck you," she whispers, but there's no heat behind it.

"Mmm, maybe later," I tease, nipping at her earlobe. "If you're a good girl."

She makes a noise somewhere between a gasp and a growl, and it shoots straight to my cock.

I pull back just enough to look her in the eye. "But for now, we have business to discuss."

I trace my thumb over her lower lip, smearing the blood there. Hers and mine.

"You're going to help me, Laura," I say, my voice low and commanding. "And in return, I'll give you everything you've ever wanted."

Her eyes search mine, looking for the catch. "And what's that?"

I smile, slow and dangerous. "Me, of course."

She rolls her eyes, a scoff escaping her lips. "You know, you could've just asked me nicely. Ever heard of texting?" Her hands press against my chest, a feeble attempt to push me away.

But there's a flicker in her gaze, a hint of desire that she can't quite hide. It's gone in an instant, replaced by a scowl.

"Why... why kidnap me?" The word slips from her, laced with anger yet tinged with curiosity.

"Well..." I hesitate, knowing the dangerous truth that she may have other enemies lurking in the shadows. But now is not the time to reveal it. *Not yet.* There's a puzzle from last night that demands solving first.

Her next words throw me for a loop, totally unexpected.

"Wait... no way, but... but are you seriously telling me you're head over heels for me?" The words tumble out of her mouth before she can stop them.

I tilt my head back, eyebrows raised, biting back a laugh.

"I mean, we had an amazing night together, but did you really have to resort to kidnapping me and changing my clothes? Is this some kind of twisted joke?" she questions.

*Amazing? Oh, sweet kiska, you haven't seen anything yet.*

"And... where are my clothes?" she asks, her eyes narrowing.

I shrug, nonchalant. "Gone. The maids disposed of them."

"Gone? Why on earth would they do that?"

"Ksenia's orders. She can't stand anything she deems unsightly," I explain, deadpan. "Ksenia's tastes are... specific."

She gives me a look like I've sprouted another head.

"How can you not see the madness in this? Kidnapping me, dressing me up like some doll in an overly plush robe?" Her voice rises in bafflement.

Okay, I have to admit, from her perspective, this must sound batshit crazy. But fuck, it's amusing watching her try to process it all.

I can't look away from her; she's fucking gorgeous. The way her body fills out that robe consumes my mind with thoughts of fucking her raw, pounding into her until she screams my name. I want to toss her onto the sofa and leave bruises on her skin as I ravage her until she begs for mercy. I can't stop imagining all the ways I could make her moan and writhe beneath me, my hands gripping her hips as I thrust deep inside of her. I want to spank her until she cries out in pleasure, then continue until she's a trembling mess.

*Suka, focus, man. You're acting like you've never seen a woman before.*

"I'm not a toy for you to play with," she hisses through clenched teeth.

I smirk, tracing a finger along her jawline. "No, you're not. You're so much more than that."

She shivers under my touch, her skin flushing pink. "What... what do you want from me?"

"Sit down, Laura," I say, my voice low but firm.

"Make me," she challenges, tempting me even more.

My cock throbs in response as I fight to calm myself down and regain control over my primal urges.

My lips hover just inches from hers, and I can sense the fear and desire emanating from her in waves. My voice drops into a low growl as I whisper, "If you keep up that attitude, you'll get a nice pussy-spanking *kiska*." The thought alone makes my body tremble with carnal anticipation, my hands itching to deliver the punishment she craves.

Her eyes widen in shock, but she obediently takes a seat on the sofa, knowing who's in control here.

I smirk. This round, *just like every other,* belongs to me.

"Now," I continue, trying to steer our interaction onto more even ground, "I think we can be of use to each other."

"Use to each other, how?" Confusion laces her voice, her brows knitting together.

"Looks like you're drowning in debt, *kiska*." I point out. We lock eyes, and I say, "And I'm in need of a wife."

I watch as she parts her lips, then clamps them shut.

Her eyelashes, long and curled, beat a frantic rhythm, mirroring the shock that's probably ricocheting through her brain.

"Are you…? Are you fucking kidding me?" The words tumble out of her in disbelief, her eyes wide with a mix of confusion and anger. "Who's pulling your strings for this kind of sick joke?"

"I don't have time for jokes, *kiska*." I lock eyes with her, letting the silence stretch, a muscle ticking in my jaw from the effort of keeping my cool. "Believe it or not, I can help you clear your debts, refurbish the bookstore," I say. "Reinstate your insurance plan…"

She scoffs, her disbelief hanging thick between us. "Right, and I suppose next you'll claim you're some kind of billionaire mafia kingpin with a soft spot for damsels in distress?"

"Yes, but let's get one thing straight—I don't do 'soft spots.' I make deals. And right now, you're in a prime position to strike one with me.

"Uh, you're joking," she blurts out, her voice shaking a bit with fear and a hint of challenge.

Then her eyebrows furrow in confusion.

"Wait, so you're telling me you *are* like some big mafia boss, right? And I'm supposed to be the queen of England?" she scoffs, clearly not buying it. "I don't get what you're playing at, but kidnapping me? You're just asking for trouble…"

I can't help but chuckle at her naivety. "Oh, little firecracker," my voice is dripping with condescension, "what kind of trouble do you think a man like me fears?"

She's visibly shaken but trying to mask it with anger. "I couldn't care less if you're running for president next, but seriously, just find my clothes and let me go, will you? I won't spill the beans to anyone," she says.

I lean in, a sly smile playing on my lips. "You think it's that simple? Just walk out and pretend none of this ever happened? *Kiska*, you're not going anywhere," I tell her. My gaze locks on her, making it crystal clear that arguing with me isn't an option.

Her eyes widen in horror, the realization dawning on her. "But… my friends, they'll notice I'm missing. They'll call the cops."

I arch an eyebrow, amused. "And you think the police will come looking for you?" My smirk widens. "*Kiska*, you don't even know what you're up against."

"I… I…" Laura starts, her voice wavering.

I don't give her the chance. My gaze fixed firmly on hers, I cut in sharply, "No '*I*s,' Laura. It's simple. If you value your one and only friend, Serena Flores, and her little family," I settle onto the leather sofa in front of her, leaning forward slightly, "you'll do what I ask you to do."

*Blyad*!

It feels weird, twisting my gut, using her best friend as leverage. I know it's a dirty move, a low blow, but it's what I've got to do to make this happen.

She opens her mouth, then closes it, the fight draining out of her. I've hit a nerve.

"See, Laura, you're in a much deeper mess than you realize," I say, my tone softening just a fraction. "But I'm offering you a way out. A deal."

She's clueless, sitting there with those wide, innocent eyes, not realizing the mess she's almost stepped into. Last night, someone else was prowling around her apartment, *someone not us.* If I hadn't shown up when I did, she would've been snatched up before she even knew what hit her. The guy bolted the second he saw my men, slipping away like a shadow. Clearly a pro, the way he vanished into thin air.

*But who the fuck sent that guy?*

I feel a knot of confusion in my gut. There's something about Laura that doesn't add up.

*And I have a feeling she doesn't know anything about it.*

"What kind of deal?" She swallows hard, her eyes darting around the room, seeking an escape that doesn't exist.

I stop my hand right before touching her face, close but not quite there. She tries to pull away, even tries to hit my hand away, but I grab her wrist before she can.

"Listen closely." I keep my voice steady. "You've got debt. I need a wife for a year." I look at her straight, making sure she gets it.

"Marry me for one year, and all your debt goes away. Simple as that."

# Chapter 20

*Laura*

**I MUST'VE** suddenly gone deaf because there's no way my ears are working right.

Mr. One-Night-Stand turned kidnapper, pitching marriage like it's a business deal.

*Three, two, one.* I fill my lungs with air.

"Victor," I say his name.

"Yes, Laura."

"Let go of me." My voice is firmer now. "Please."

The room goes quiet, the kind of quiet that feels like a buildup to a storm. My eyes are flickering nervously under his intense stare.

Then, abruptly, the fierceness in his eyes dims as though someone flipped a switch. He lets go and leans back. "I apologize." He breathes in deep, a visible effort to rein in whatever storm brews inside him.

It's like watching a wolf decide not to bite. Utterly bizarre and kind of terrifying.

Breaking the tension, I blurt out, "Sorry for being rude, but are you out of your freaking mind?"

I'm eyeballing him, trying to play it cool. Sagging into the leather sofa, I say, "Okay, let's pretend for a second that I'm not totally wigging out. You'll clear *all* my debts."

"Yes."

"And you'll restore my bookstore?"

"Yes." He nods like he's asking me to pass the salt.

"And in exchange, I'll need to… marry you for a year."

Taking a sharp breath, he clearly struggles to maintain his composure, pinching the bridge of his nose in silent frustration.

"Yes, Laura, I don't enjoy repeating myself," he states firmly. "I'm not asking, I'm telling. This is how it's going to be."

Ignoring his irritation, I give him a smile, the kind you give a kid who's telling a tall tale.

"I'm flattered, really. But there's a wedding in your grand plan. I'm *already* married. Too bad, now you'll just need to find someone else to be your *wife*."

I'm scanning his face for any telltale signs, but his face is stone-cold.

"Hello, earth to Victor?" I try to snag his attention, but he's striding over to his desk. God, he's somehow managed to get even more good-looking since I last saw him. My gaze trails after him like it's got a mind of its own.

*Seriously, who's built like that?*

There's an intensity about him today that's hard to miss. He's wearing this white shirt, casually unbuttoned at the top, showing off just enough to tease. His hair's got this perfect, I-don't-care-but-I-totally-do look.

*Jesus, Laur.*

I shift uncomfortably, crossing my legs. This is ridiculous. I shouldn't be noticing these things, not now. But Lord, why does he look like he just walked straight off of one of those steamy book covers?

*Cut it out, Laur, focus.*

I watch Victor pick up a brown file from his desk. He lifts his gaze; his gray eyes catch mine. For a moment, I think I see… *No, it can't be… A hint of sympathy?*

"No, *kiska*, that's not marriage. You got *played*," he says, his voice cold again.

Victor strides over. I try to swallow, but my throat is dry.

"You got played for cash in a scam and sham by the man you *thought* was David Gardner."

"Wha-what?" I'm struggling to comprehend. "What are you talking about?"

He lays the file down in front of me. "The man you believed is your husband is just a fiction; his real name is *Dave Jankowski*."

"Th-that's not true," I stutter; everything in me feels like it's crashing down. "Stop… stop… lying."

"No, Laura, your marriage to David is a lie."

I let out a nervous laugh, shaking my head in denial. "No… you don't know… you don't know what you are talking about." I search his face for clues, clues that all of this is just a fucking joke.

He leans closer, and the scent of cedarwood from him envelops me. It's a weird thing to notice when my entire life is unraveling.

"I know exactly what I'm talking about."

My stomach twists into knots.

*Stop. Please.*

"David Gardner is *dead*."

"What the hell are you saying?" Anger flares, but it's drowned out by confusion and fear.

*I knew David cheated and scammed all my money… But dead?*

I'm biting my lips. Hard. Trying to process everything. But I can't; nothing seems to make sense anymore.

"The *real* David died five years ago," he continues, his voice deep and sure. "You, Laura Anne Thompson, are a victim of marriage fraud."

It's like my brain refuses to process his words.

Victor flicks open the folder, presenting it to me as if unveiling a verdict.

I reach out, hand shaking as I sift through the documents—the irrefutable proof in photos, reports, and a death certificate.

I stare at it.

My eyes keep darting back to the name printed so clearly on the paper: **David Gardner. Born in 1966, fifty-eight years old at the time of his death. Cause of death: A DUI accident.**

I'm gripping the death certificate, my fingers nearly crumpling the paper.

Everything in the room seems to tilt as I flip through the police reports. Each one is a stark reality check, outlining frauds and scams, all tied back to the man I called my husband.

"This can't be right..." My voice is a faint whisper. I can't tear my gaze away from the photos that follow. There he is, "David," or whoever he really is, with dyed hair, a cap pulled low. He's trying not to be recognized, but it's clearly him. And there's Polly, always a shadow in the background.

My hands shake as I sift through more photos—motel entries, dark alley dealings. It's like peering into a parallel universe where my husband is a ghost, a phantom I never really knew.

"Laura," I hear Victor say my name. "I'm the only way out for you now."

Victor nonchalantly pulls out his phone and commands, "Come in."

Seconds later, the door opens, and two men in suits stride in.

"Wha-what's going on?" My voice is shaky.

The first man, exuding an air of strict professionalism, extends a hand toward me. "Ms. Thompson, I'm Andrew Taylor, legal counsel for Morozov Corporation. I'm here to discuss your marriage contract with Mr. Morozov."

My head spins. "Marriage contract?" Without fully realizing why, my hand moves on its own to meet Andrew's in a handshake.

Andrew offers a thin smile. "Yes, given the circumstances, it is necessary. You'll find everything in order." He hands me a thick document.

I glance over at Victor, who remains silent, his gaze fixed on me.

"What the hell is this insane situation?" I blurt out.

I glance beyond Andrew to the other man stationed like a guard by the door, an unspoken barrier between me and any thought of escape. The towering figure with a broad chest sports a rugged look, complete with a beard and sharp, blue eyes that seem to pierce through me. There's a smirk playing on his lips, one that irks me deeply.

I'm staring at Victor, then at Andrew, disbelief clouding my judgment. "But... but I'm a married woman." I may have been duped by David, but that marriage certificate must mean something, surely?

"Not anymore, Ms. Thompson." Andrew calmly seats himself across from me, sliding a sheaf of papers across the table. My hands tremble as I pick them up, my eyes scanning the title incredulously. "Divorce Decree Finalized," it reads, official stamps and signatures littering the bottom of the page.

My heart skips. "But how is this... even possible?"

"Let's just say we have our ways with certain... judicial processes." Andrew forces a smile at me.

I stare at Victor "Are you fucking insane?" I stand up abruptly.

I try to steady myself as Victor moves closer, his aura exuding a mix of danger and control. He takes a seat next to me.

"*Kiska*, what's *insane* is that you married a man when you have no clue who he really is," he says, his voice low and steady.

I can't hold back the tears that start to flow. He's right. My entire marriage, everything, has been a fucking lie.

"But... why me?" I manage to ask through sobs, wiping away tears. "Why...?"

"Because," Victor's tone is icy as he tilts my face up to his, "you're just a pawn. And now? You're Morozov Bratva's property."

# Chapter 21

*Victor*

**I WATCH** her.

Her face drains of all warmth, her once rosy-pink lips now pale and trembling with fear. I can't help but feel a surge of pleasure at the sight, knowing that this is just how I like it.

*Blyad, I want to taste those quivering lips, to savor her fear and make it my own.*

"Brat…va?" she stutters out, those lips of hers parting slightly in shock.

"Yes. Bratva," I confirm, letting go of her face finally.

She squints. "As in, mafia and gangster, like… the Godfather? Scarface?" Attempting to hold back tears, she ends up sniffling, her breath hitching with each stifled sob.

"Exactly like that. But we're the real deal. Not some Hollywood fantasy." I let the words sink in, watching her process it.

Nervously, she runs her tongue over her lips and struggles to swallow the growing lump in her throat. "This has got to be a joke. It just has to be," she whispers, confusion etched across her pretty face.

I let her process my words for a moment, watching as her eyes widen in disbelief and realization. "It's not just a simple con, Laura," I say sharply, making sure she grasps the gravity of the situation. "Dave Jankowski was deep in debt with us, the Morozov Bratva. He owed us a fortune."

Laura's gaze sharpens, something clicking behind those eyes. She's got that look, the one where she's connecting dots, her lips press into a thin line, holding back a storm of words or maybe just a flood of questions.

Her voice trembles as she speaks. "David… he was involved with the mafia, wasn't he?"

"Yes," I confirm coldly. "And he owed us two million dollars. And when he couldn't pay up, he used you as collateral."

"What?" She gasps, her hand flying up to cover her mouth, eyes wide with shock. "Wha-what does that mean?"

I can't help but feel a thrill watching her fear slowly mount.

"It means," I say, my voice low and steady, "he sold you to us, Laura." My eyes fix on hers, not missing a single flicker of emotion that crosses her face. "Your life now belongs to the Morozov Bratva."

Watching her fear grow is a perverse pleasure; it's the kind of control I'm used to.

"He... sold me?" Her voice cracks a bit, disbelief written all over her face.

"That's what he did." I lean in, making sure she gets every word. "To him, you were just a way to clear his debts. Nothing personal."

"Are you fucking insane?" She's almost yelling now, her face a mix of shock and anger. "How is it my responsibility to pay off David's debts? This doesn't make any sense. I shouldn't be the one paying for his mistakes," Laura snaps. "You can't just claim someone's life like it's yours to take," she fires, her eyes darting around, from me to Andrew, then to Misha.

I stride back to my leather chair, the reality of our world versus hers needing clarification.

"In our world, little firecracker, the normal rules don't apply. The legal world you cling to, it's not here. In the Morozov Bratva, debts are not just numbers. They bind families, fates, and, yes, even the innocent. David's debts, they're yours now. That's how our world works."

Laura's jaw tightens, a telltale sign of the storm brewing within her.

Andrew steps forward, sliding the contract toward Laura. "Ms. Thompson, it's in your best interest to sign these now." She tries to shove it away, putting some real force behind it.

But Andrew, unfazed, quickly catches the contract before it falls. With a steady hand, he places it right back in front of her. "This isn't about bullying. It's your way out."

"You can't just force someone to marry you!" She's got her fists balled up tight, breathing like she's run a mile. Her eyes are all fired up, staring me down.

*God, she's sexy when she's angry. But it's time to remind her who's in control here.*

"Listen," I whisper fiercely, "this isn't a fairy tale, and I'm not the prince coming to rescue you. But I am the man who can make all your problems disappear. Poof." I snap my fingers, a sharp crack in the silence of the room.

She looks down at the contract again, the numbers probably dancing in her head. Renovated bookstore, debt-free life... It's a hell of a golden carrot to dangle.

"You can't just buy everything, Victor," she murmurs.

"You really think so?" The corner of my mouth twitches upward in a smirk.

"I... yes." She pauses, chewing on her lip, clearly wrestling with the decision, her eyes flickering with uncertainty.

"You really don't have a choice." I take a slow drag of my cigar. "Sign the contract, or things get much worse. You have no choice."

"No choice? Watch me." She's moving toward the door with a newfound determination.

But Misha simply steps in front of her, blocking her path completely. "Run, and your friend Serena and her family will pay the price." His gaze never wavers from hers as he moves closer, forcing Laura to take steps backward.

"You!" She spins around to face me, anger and fear mixing on her tear-stained cheeks. "Leave Serena alone!" she shouts.

*Ah, there it is—the fear I want to see.*

"Sign the papers, Laura," I state coldly, holding out the contract for her to take.

She bristles at my words, her body tensed like a cornered animal. "You're a monster!" she growls.

"Perhaps." I shrug indifferently. "But I'm a monster who keeps his word."

The glint of fear in her eyes only fuels my satisfaction. I turn to Misha with a cold command, "Bring her back here."

Laura's body trembles as Misha grips her arm tightly and leads her back to where Andrew sits. "Who the hell are you?!" she barks, her eyes filled with resentful defiance and fear.

"You can call me a wolf, a beast, or anything else you desire," he snarls. "But now you need to sign the fucking contract like the boss asked you to." He pushes her toward the sofa where Andrew sits, his hand firm on her arm.

Laura hesitates, her eyes flitting between the contract and Andrew's stoic face, then back to me.

"Ms. Thompson," Andrew starts, clearing his throat for emphasis, "by signing this contract, you're agreeing to all our terms and conditions."

"I never agreed to any of this!" She's boiling with rage, her anger sharp, fear trembling through her.

"It's your best bet," I say, flicking a glance her way.

"I fucking *HATE* you," she spits out, her eyes blazing with anger. She knows she's cornered, no way out, and it's all directed at me.

I shrug, playing it cool. But fuck, hearing her say she hates me? It's like a goddamn knife to the gut.

*What the fuck? Why do I even care?*

Trembling, she carefully turns to the contract's final page, signing her name on the dotted line, a single tear sliding down her cheek.

But she knows there is nothing else she can do.

# Chapter 22

*Victor*

**I SINK** into the worn leather of my father's old chair, the one I've coveted since I was a boy. It feels different now, heavier somehow, weighted with the responsibility of the Morozov name. But it's a weight I'm ready to bear, a mantle I've been preparing for all my life.

Ksenia leans against the doorway of my office, her arms crossed, an eyebrow arched in that way she does when she's about to delve into something she thinks is a bad idea.

"So, Laura Anne Thompson? That's your brilliant plan?"

I give a nonchalant shrug, not bothering to glance away from my screen. "She fits the bill, Ksenia. It's all about timing."

Casting a quick glance at Ksenia, I catch her eyebrow shooting up further, disbelief painting her expression. "You're paying off her debts and orchestrating her divorce. You're more sentimental than I thought, Victor."

I turn my attention back to the computer screen. "It's convenient," I respond, my voice flat. "She's a clean slate, no ties to our circles."

Ksenia laughs. "Convenient for whom, Victor? You're about to shackle yourself to a common girl. This is not one of your typical games."

*Zaebis, Ksenia never lets anything go.*

I lean back in my chair. "You think I'm a fool, *Ksyusha*?" I lock eyes with her. "I need a wife; she needs a way out. It's a simple trade."

Ksenia, always the calm in the storm, watches me, her gaze sharp. "You're playing with fire, *Vitya*. This woman, Laura... She's a time bomb. You're binding her to the Bratva over a debt she didn't even know existed."

I scoff, rolling my eyes. "Please, it's not like I'm marrying her for love. It's a business transaction. It's just a deal to make sure Papa gets his surgery. Doesn't matter who the *bride* is."

Ksenia shakes her head. "And what happens when this 'business transaction' goes south? Bringing some common girl into our world is a stupid move. She won't last a week."

"She'll learn to swim," I retort coldly, the nastiness in my tone unmistakable. "Laura Anne Thompson's life as she knew it is over. She's part of the Morozov Bratva now, whether she likes it or not."

Ksenia's eyes narrow. "And what about you, Victor? Are you ready for what this means? Tying yourself to someone who could be your downfall?"

I stand, towering over her, my presence dominating the space. "It'll never happen, *Ksyusha*."

She studies me for a moment. Her gaze lingers on me, a sinister smirk unfolding across her lips. "Mark my words," she hisses, "if she ever becomes a danger to our family, I won't hesitate to eliminate her."

SLAM!

My hand crashes down on the table, the sound echoing off the walls. It's a rare loss of control from me, but Ksenia's words hit me like daggers.

"Don't you dare question my loyalty, Ksenia. You know damn well how important this alliance is for our family." I can feel my muscles tensing, ready to strike back at her insults.

A normal person would have pissed themselves from fear by now, but not Ksenia.

She just stares back, unflinching, that damn smirk playing on her lips. "That's a big reaction for something you don't care about… little brother," she taunts, her gaze drilling into mine. "Don't let your feelings get in the way."

*Blyad!*

"There's no fucking room for feelings here," I snap, my anger barely contained.

Ksenia's cold gaze momentarily flickers with something akin to surprise before she masks it with her usual frost. It's a game to her, but I'm not playing.

I inhale sharply. "For fuck's sake, Ksenia," I growl, my patience wearing thin. "Just focus on the wedding! It's in three days, and I want the entire underworld talking about it."

Her lips twitch; not quite a smile, more a sardonic curl. "Oh, they'll talk, alright," she replies, her voice dripping with unspoken threats. "But remember, Victor, she's your responsibility. Any misstep, any danger she brings…"

I cut her off, "Don't fucking test me, Ksenia. She's soon to be my wife and mine to worry about. Touch her, and you'll regret it."

For a split second, surprise flickers across Ksenia's usually unreadable face.

Then, as quickly as it came, it's gone, replaced once again by that chilling calm. "As you wish, little brother," she concedes, though her eyes tell me this conversation is far from over.

# Chapter 23

*Laura*

"WHERE THE hell is this place?"

My mind races, thinking about escape, but the mansion stretches so far that I can't even see where it ends.

I pull my eyes away from the crazy view outside the big window, right here in this room that Misha, the menacing figure, has me locked in.

*Fuck. Is there even a way out of this massive place?*

Then, footsteps. My heart kicks up a notch. I whip around, bracing for someone to storm in.

But no one comes.

The footsteps fade out, leaving me alone again. It's just the maids, chatting in whispers too low to catch, rushing off somewhere fast.

The doorknob rattles as I jiggle it frantically, but it doesn't budge. Locked. "Fuck," I mutter under my breath, slamming my palm against the polished wood in frustration. Turning around, I survey the room again with a growing sense of dread.

"This is crazy," I say to the empty room. "I can't believe this is happening."

I shut my eyes, counting to three, half-expecting everything to change.

*Three... two... one.*

But when I look again, nothing's different. Still trapped here.

Drawing in a long breath.

"Okay, deep breath," I mutter, using that old trick I perfected as a kid—deep breathing to stave off panic whenever Dad's temper flared or when missing Mommy got too much.

But this?

This is a whole new level of crazy. A part of me is actually relieved to be done with David Gardner, but jumping from a sham marriage to being essentially "owned" by the mafia? This is some next-level insanity.

I take in another three deep breaths by the window, then turn to scan the room, and it's nothing like I expected—it's actually kind of *homey*.

Not at all what I'd expect from a mafia lord—if I even know what that's supposed to look like.

The place is dressed in creams and rich wood tones, with a fireplace you could camp in and a chandelier that catches the light, scattering it like tiny stars against the cream. The sun blasts through the huge windows, throwing gold across everything, lighting up the place like some high-end catalog shoot.

*God, how big is this room? It's at least ten times the size of my own bedroom.*

There's a staircase curving up to the second floor, classy but not over-the-top. I have no intention of exploring upstairs. Who knows what or who I'd find?

*No, thank you.*

I let myself fall into one of the couches, and it's like landing on a cloud—if clouds were made of the most expensive materials on earth.

I flash back to Victor's stone-cold business face as he slides the contract across to me. "Read it, understand it."

"Sure thing, jerk," I mutter, not like he is here to spank me.

*Good God, Laur, you shouldn't wish for that.*

Stress is written all over me; I can feel it in the weight of my chest. I rub my temples, drawing in a deep, shaky breath, looking at the contract still clutched in my hand, its stark black letters spelling my new destiny.

Labeling me officially as *"Contractual Spouse of Victor Morozov under Morozov Bratva Terms."*

I scoff. "Contractual spouse or glorified hostage?"

But it's not just about me.

Serena's safety is the real contract here, the one that's written in blood, not ink.

"Fuckers!" I spit out.

The way Misha talked about Serena… his words were chillingly precise. He knew their Friday routine, down to the damn hour they'd be at Target picking up whatever for little Lucas.

This isn't a joke, not some scare tactic. They know. They actually know where she is, and they're not above dragging her into this hell.

*I have to do this. For Serena, for her family. Because if I don't...*

The contract crumples in my fist, knuckles blanching. Just thinking about the risk to Serena and her family amps up my anxiety.

"God, I really messed up," I mutter, feeling like my chest is trapped in a tight grip, making it hard to breathe without letting tears escape. "If they get hurt because of me... I don't even know how I'd live with that."

Every fiber of my being is jittery, teetering on the edge of a breakdown.

"Just get through it, Laura," I mumble, pressing a hand against my chest, trying to quell the rising panic before I flip through the contract, determined to grasp every rule set to dominate my life.

I recline, the couch's cushions a small comfort as I stretch the contract before me, the tiny print blurring into lines of my impending reality.

*Seriously?*

"Okay, listen to this one," I announce to the empty room. "The clause here states that I am granted the liberty of leaving the house for a maximum duration of not more than *five hours* at a time."

*How generous of them!*

"Great, I feel like Cinderella, if Cinderella was trapped in a mafia tale with no fairy godmother in sight," I grumble, chewing on my nail.

Sitting up straighter, I continue to read out loud, "Furthermore, such outings are subject to prior approval and shall be accompanied at all times by no less than one (1) designated security personnel.

"Because, you know, heaven forbid I try to enjoy a latte in peace." I snort.

Letting out a long, slow breath, I feel my shoulders drop as the tension drains away.

I thought I'd be locked up in a dungeon; instead, I'm allowed to see my friends and family?

*Should I be grateful?*

I turn the page, and for a moment, my thoughts can't keep pace with what I'm seeing. Printed clearly, a condition so outrageous, it sends my mind spinning.

My gaze snaps back to the words, sure I've misread.

But no, the numbers glare back at me, bold and unyielding.

"This has to be a joke." I slap a hand over my mouth, shocked. After a beat, I pull the contract closer, trying to make sense of the crazy figure printed on it.

**Monthly Allowance and Shopping Provision Clause**

**"The Husband agrees to provide The Wife with a monthly allowance of Two Hundred Thousand Dollars ($200,000) for her personal use and shopping needs, in line with his status. A personal account will be set up for The Wife, with a payment card for full access to these funds, deposited on the first business day of each month."**

My hand flies to my face, rubbing my eyes once, twice, thrice, as if that could somehow change the numbers on the page.

"In line with his *status*?" I echo, my voice a mix of incredulity and a slight hint of amusement.

"Does that mean diamond-studded toothpicks and gold-plated... what, everything?"

I let out a low, mocking laugh, shaking my head with a bemused chuckle.

Well, if this isn't a whole new level of madness, I don't know what is. My brain is struggling to make sense of this.

This has to be a typo, right? Yet, I doubt they'd make a mistake like this.

"Is this their idea of pocket money?" I whisper. "Two hundred grand? Shopping for what, a small country?" I half-shout, disbelief making my eyes widen. I reread the clause, but it stubbornly remains the same.

Rubbing my eyes again, I lean closer, as if proximity could somehow alter the reality of the figures before me.

"This is *real*," I utter, reading the clause again and then once more for good measure. My hand unconsciously covers my mouth as I let out a low whistle, the absurdity of it all making my head spin.

"And here I was, worrying about paying rent on time," I say with a laugh that's more disbelief than amusement. The thought of that kind of money, just for me, every month, is wilder than anything I could've imagined. It's like I've stepped into an alternate universe where numbers have lost all meaning.

Shaking my head, I push the contract aside for a moment, needing a break from its surreal promises. "Well, at least shopping won't be an issue," I quip.

As my pulse races, I try to steady my breath, not wanting my heart to burst through. "Calm down, Laur," I whisper, urging calmness into the chaos of my thoughts.

My focus returns to the contract.

"**You shall not ask anything about Morozov Corp's business,**" I read out loud.

*Ha, like I'd ever want to ask about his business!*

What do I care about how many people he's offed or how many women he's kidnapped to play house with?

*Ridiculous.*

Then my eyebrows shoot up to my hairline, and I can feel my face heat up, reading the next line:

**"Both parties, by signing below, agree to share living quarters in the same room. This setup is part of the agreement and must be followed for the entire length of the contract."**

"Wait, you mean we're sharing a room?" Panic flares up, half-tempted to yank at my hair, a desperate move to keep from spiraling. But I force my hands down, clenching them into fists instead.

And then, the grand finale of absurdity hits me. My eyes snag on the last line.

**"Both parties agree not to develop romantic feelings or engage in a love relationship."**

I laugh sharply. "Yeah, right, as if I'd fall for my captor," I say, rolling my eyes. The entire situation is just absurd—the lavish allowance, the strict rules, and now, a clause about not falling in love. "Only in a mafia contract would love be listed like a grocery item," I whisper under my breath, shaking my head in disbelief.

But this whole thing... It's not as dire as I feared, though.

All of a sudden, the door creaks open unannounced.

First, it's the scent that hits me—a mix of jasmine and something fiercely expensive—it's *her.*

My head snaps up, my entire body going rigid as she strides in.

My mind races, trying to place her in the Morozov family puzzle, but my thoughts scatter as she stands before me.

She enters with measured steps, her stare drilling into me, icy and sharp.

"Don't do that," she snaps, catching me biting my nails again.

I jerk my hands away, feeling like a kid caught stealing cookies. "So-sorry," I stammer, dropping my hands to my lap.

*Damn, she's terrifying.*

Her gaze sweeps over me, cold and calculating, from the top of my head down to the soles of my feet. I feel her taking inventory, noting every detail, every reaction. Finally, landing on the contract sprawled across my lap.

"Looks like you've hit the jackpot, haven't you?" she remarks, a sardonic edge to her voice.

Caught off guard, I fidget uncomfortably. "Uh, well… I wasn't exactly expecting *this*," I admit, voice a notch too high.

She's got me feeling smaller than small. My nails find my lip in a nervous tic.

"Drop that nasty habit," she says, her gaze slicing through me, taking stock of every twitch and flinch. With a casual flick, she locks her arms across her chest.

My hands fall to my sides, quick and obedient, shrinking under her stare.

*Fucking great, now she's channeling my dad.*

I bite back a curse, yanking my hand from my mouth like it's suddenly gone rogue.

Then, Ksenia snaps her fingers, and the door swings open. In stride a bunch of women dressed in gray, white, and black.

A tall, stunning blond charges in, gripping her makeup kit as if it's her armor, her heels clicking on the floor like gunfire. Right on her heels, another woman, her hair yanked back into a strict bun, drags a rack brimming with dresses.

"What… now?" I ask, turning back to Ksenia for some clue… any clue.

Ksenia gives me a disapproving look. "Time for a bath. You look like something we'd scrape off the floor." She nods at the maids to take action.

*...And whose brilliant idea was it to kidnap me, huh?*

Before my mind even has a chance to catch up, I'm suddenly being dragged by a group of women who seem to know their way around my body, stripping me down like I'm just another task on their to-do list.

*This can't be happening.*

"Wait, what the hell?" My voice spikes in alarm, clutching at the robe I'm barely in.

Suddenly, I'm swarmed by hands, quick and practiced, stripping away my clothes with alarming efficiency.

"Stop!" The command bursts from me, filling the room, but it's futile—I'm left standing there, completely naked.

"What the hell is this?" I scream, my voice trembling with fear and anger as I try to cover myself with shaking hands.

"I see why Victor likes you," Ksenia smirks, her eyes scanning my naked body with amusement.

*This woman is pure evil.*

I cannot believe this. Left standing naked, the focus of a room full of strangers.

"Make her presentable," Ksenia commands, her tone dismissive, like I'm nothing more than a project.

"*Da, mem,*" one of the maids responds, her voice devoid of any emotion.

"Hey, let me go!" I struggle, but it's like trying to shake off steel grips. "This is insane; do you hear me?" Fury and shock mix in my veins. "You can't do this!" I yell. "What is all of this for?" I manage to sputter out in confusion.

Suddenly, a bathrobe is thrown over me, a brief reprieve from the exposure. But before I can even tie the sash, I'm being pulled upstairs by two maids, each holding an arm, their grip firm.

"Get your hands off me!" I demand, my feet dragging against the plush carpet as I'm herded upstairs like cattle. "Fucking stop this madness!"

"Presentable for what?" The words stumble out, confusion and anger swirling as I turn my attention back to Ksenia. I press for answers as we ascend the grand staircase. "Answer me! For what?"

"For the *Pakhan*," she says casually as she flips through dresses with the blond woman by her side. "You're meeting our father tonight."

The word "father" echoes in my head, mingling with the ominous title "*Pakhan*."

*Meaning... boss of bosses.*

My mind races, trying to piece together this new, terrifying reality.

*Yeah, I read enough mafia romance to learn the meaning of these words. Didn't know it was educational!* I think to myself, rolling my eyes.

*And fantastic. Just how many fucking bogeymen am I scheduled to meet today?*

"The wedding is in three days," Ksenia announces coldly, a statement that sends my heart into a freefall. "And you have a lot to learn."

"Okay, someone's got to tell me what's going on here. Please." My plea is desperate, the situation spiraling beyond my grasp. "I didn't think the wedding would be so soon!"

*Crap! How did I end up here?*

Ksenia strides over; she smells like power.

When she comes too close to me, I flinch.

"You're not telling anyone about the contract you have with Victor," she hisses close to my face. "Not a single soul, you understand?"

My eyes snap wide, and for a second, I can't find the words. I purse my lips, trying to wrap my head around what she's saying. "Yes, ma'am," slips out.

Stepping back, Ksenia watches me silently before finally speaking up again. "I've changed my mind. I don't know what my brother sees in you," she sneers.

"Just try not to die before the contract is up."

# Chapter 24

*Laura*

**PUSHED INTO** the bathroom, the door bangs shut behind me.

Ksenia's parting shot echoes in my head.

*"I don't know what my brother sees in you. Just try not to die before the contract is up."*

Leaning against the door, I let out a silent scoff.

"Trust me, Ksenia, the feeling's mutual. I've no idea what your brother sees in me, either. And dying wasn't on my to-do list today." A snort breaks free as I consider the sibling connection.

"Great, so she's Victor's sister. Makes sense. They're both drop-dead gorgeous and have the same kind, charming personality," I huff quietly.

*Wow.*

The reality of my situation hits me like a bucket of ice water. Kidnapped, divorced, and now engaged to a mafia lord—all in the span of what, a day?

I shove my hair back from my face, fingers trembling slightly, trying to anchor myself to the moment.

*Ew.* My hair is a tangled thicket, infused with yesterday's fear and turmoil. I haven't had the chance to scrub away the remnants of yesterday's chaos since I woke up in Eli's room.

Suddenly, I remember hearing *David's*—no, *Dave's*—whatever his damn name is, voice on the phone before I got kidnapped in my own home.

*Has he been watching me this whole time?*

Disgust washes over me like a second skin. It's all just too much. Pushing that creepy thought to the back of my mind, I force out a deep, steadying breath. My gaze finally drifts upwards, taking in the luxury of the bathroom once more.

*Holy cow.*

It's fancy in here, way fancier than anywhere I should be. White marble everywhere, looking expensive and cold. There's a huge tub under a window; most likely costs more than I earn in a month.

There's a sink that's too pretty to spit toothpaste into and a bunch of soaps and stuff that probably smell like money.

Two plush, white bathrobes hang on a hook by the door, a big glass thing with more showerheads than I've got fingers. Looks like it could blast the dirt off a dinosaur.

*Jesus.* At least I'm alone for the first time in what feels like forever.

I press my ear against the door, straining for any sound of the maids.

Silence greets me. But I know that they are right outside.

Waiting.

Plotting their next move in the "Make Laura Presentable" production ordered by Ksenia. The thought makes me want to lock the door and hide in the tub.

A sudden knock at the door yanks me from my brief respite. The voice that follows is unmistakably Russian, tinged with a coldness that brooks no argument.

"Please hurry. Your presence is expected at dinner in two hours. We need to start getting you ready," the voice instructs, its authority clear even through the closed door.

I straighten up, steeling myself.

*For fuck's sake.*

"Alright, just give me a moment," I call back, though I sound a lot less confident than I'd like.

I glance at myself in the mirror, trying to muster some semblance of the person I need to be to face whatever's next. My reflection stares back, a mix of determination and nerves.

"Two hours," I remind myself.

I quickly strip off the bathrobe and step into the shower, cranking up the hot water as high as I can tolerate it.

As I lather soap onto my body, I catch a whiff of soap from the nearby tray. My hand automatically reaches for it, squeezing out a tiny bit and bringing it to my nose.

*Umm…*

It smells like men's soap. *His* scent. A rugged blend of wood and spice.

A choked gasp escapes me as I remember his cock, hard and unyielding between my lips, filling me with equal parts shame and arousal.

How can my body betray me like this? Crave the touch of a man who holds me captive, who has made clear his intentions to possess me in every way imaginable?

*Laur, get a grip on yourself.*

This is not a love story; it is a deal struck with the devil himself.

The thought of sharing this bathroom with Victor makes bile rise in my throat. I can almost feel his presence looming over me, even though I am alone.

"What the fuck is wrong with me?" I mutter to myself before turning on the shower again to drown out my dirty thoughts.

I grab a bottle of shampoo and work it into my hair with more force than necessary. The suds slide down my body and swirl around my feet, carrying away some of the shame that weighs on me.

Stepping out of the shower and getting back into a bathrobe, steam clouds around me. My hair drips onto the marble floor as two maids walk in and nudge me toward the dressing table. They'd waited just outside the room, exactly as I expected.

The sight of the massive bed catches my eye—it dominates the room; the scent of lavender and sandalwood drifts from the sheets.

Tempting and sinful.

My thoughts turn to Victor yet again, his body pressed against mine as we sink into the softness of the sheets.

*Ugh, stop it! Have some self-control, damnit.*

I barely have a moment to gawk at the bed when they plant me in front of a mirror. This dressing table's as over-the-top as everything else here. While the maids fuss over my dripping hair, I hear those telltale heels.

*Click, click, click.*

Someone's coming, and they're not happy.

A woman materializes in the mirror's reflection, her beauty masking a simmering rage. Her eyes meet mine in the reflection, sharp enough to cut through steel.

"So, you're the one," she hisses, her Russian accent dripping with disdain.

I swallow hard, meeting her glare in the mirror. "I guess… I am," I reply, trying to keep my voice steady.

"You're nothing like I expected," she sneers, circling around to face me. "Victor's never had such… plain taste."

*Ouch.*

That hurts more than I'd like to admit. I bet Victor's usual type is leagues away from a "plain Laura" like me. It hits me then—she's got a thing for Victor. I'm suddenly the lead in a drama I never auditioned for.

"Well, I'm full of surprises," I shoot back, but my voice quivers, betraying me.

She rolls her eyes at me.

"Surprises? Doubtful," she retorts.

Grabbing a comb, she begins to work through my hair with more force than necessary, clearly enjoying each tug a bit too much.

"What's your name?" I ask, my jaw clenched tight, biting back the pain.

"Irina," she snaps quietly, her focus more on punishing my scalp than making introductions.

I wince as she yanks through a particularly stubborn knot. "Nice to meet you, Irina."

Ignoring me, she continues pulling and twisting my hair into a sleek, simple style that somehow manages to look elegant despite the rough handling.

She draws in a short breath. "I don't know why he chose an American girl," she mutters under her breath, probably thinking I can't hear her.

*But I do.*

"Well, I don't know why either," I retort before I can stop myself.

Irina pretends not to hear me, but I catch a slight twitch in her cheek. She abruptly pushes the chair back and hauls out a massive makeup suitcase.

I stare, wide-eyed, at the arsenal of makeup before me. "Holy... Are you painting a mural on my face or something?" I can't help but quip, eyeing the array of colors and brushes.

Irina mutters something in Russian, a clear note of annoyance in her voice, then exhales loudly, switching back to English with a sharp edge. "Eyes shut," Irina orders, not amused by my comment.

I comply, feeling the brush strokes sweep over my eyelids.

The makeover continues in tense silence, broken only by the occasional sharp command from Irina.

"Chin up."

"Eyes still."

"Hold steady."

*Why do I need to be dolled up like I'm attending the Grammy Awards ceremony?*

Finally, after what feels like an eternity in the chair, she stops.

"You're done," Irina declares abruptly, snapping her makeup case shut. I take a deep breath and open my eyes, meeting the gaze of someone I hardly recognize in the mirror.

"Wow," I can't help but let the word escape, my shock evident.

*Who the hell is this person staring back at me?*

"I look like someone else," I gasp out, still stunned. Irina's attempt to stay stern falters for a moment, and a shadow of a smile sneaks onto her face. She quickly smothers it, though, turning to signal the maids.

"Bring the dresses," she barks, shifting back to business.

Two maids approach, each bearing a dress so stunning it momentarily steals my breath. One is a sleek black number, its fabric shimmering subtly in the light, embodying elegance and mystery. The other is a nude, ethereal gown, its chiffon fabric flowing and delicate, like something out of an old, elegant painting.

"For me?" I can't help but ask.

"Of course, it is. Stand up now. We need to get you ready," she says, her tone cold and stern.

"I can dress myself," I insist, pulling away from her and locking eyes. "Please, just give me some space."

Resignation mixes with annoyance as Irina exhales sharply and mutters something in Russian to the maids, who reluctantly step back and hand me the dresses.

The fabric glides through my fingers like a silken dream. I look at the black dress; my breath catches in my throat as I glimpse the label—Chanel.

"Chanel," I repeat in disbelief, unable to believe that I am actually holding a piece of luxury fashion in my hands.

My eyes land on the other dress, the McQueen one. It's classy, and it looks fucking expensive—practically screams that I'm out of my depth. "Am I really wearing these?" I whisper to myself, the idea of it all feeling like some elaborate prank.

*Damn.*

I picture myself stumbling, a wave of chocolate ruining thousands of dollars of fabric. The thought makes me suck in a breath.

Irina's impatience is palpable, her tapping heel a metronome counting down my hesitation. "Well? Are you going to try them on or not?" Her finger jabs in the direction of the dressing room.

*Okay, princess transformation it is.*

But my so-called fairy godmother is clearly on a schedule.

I take a step toward the dressing room. A smirk dances on my lips at the thought of fleeing at midnight, my fancy attire left behind.

Just then, a small, energetic figure appears at the top of the staircase.

"Boo!" She's all giggles, twirling in her mini gown. Eli comes charging into the room like a little tornado, full of energy.

"Okay, I'm not scared of you anymore." I keep my voice light, though I half-expect Ksenia to follow her lead, but the staircase remains empty.

"Laura, you're not dressed yet?" Eli's question is more of an impatient nudge. "I'm here to bring you to dinner."

Her mother's absence is a small relief. "I don't know which dress to wear," I admit, sticking out my tongue at her.

"Laura! You're an adult!" she tries to scold me, her little face serious. "You should know everything."

*Oh, my sweet girl, if only that were true.*

"Well, sometimes the adults…" I kneel down to her level, searching for words that could bridge our worlds, "they have to make tough choices, just like kids do."

"That's okay, Laura." She nods solemnly. "Sometimes, I'm not sure…" she pauses, her face scrunching in thought, "why Yuri is sad, but I give him the biggest hugs."

I don't know who Yuri is, but I nod slightly, biting back my curiosity. "Maybe later you can tell me about Yuri."

Eli just nods, her little face beaming up again.

"Eli, darling, can you help me pick?" I gesture toward the dresses in my hands, bending down to show her.

She points eagerly at the McQueen dress, her small hand barely steady. "This one!" She beams. "It's the same color as mine!" And she twirls again, her dress fanning out around her.

"Perfect choice." I feel a flicker of excitement, a shared moment of kinship, as I head for the dressing room.

"Hurry up, Laura!" Eli's tone shifts, her inner general taking charge. "*Dedushka* is waiting."

"*Dedushka*?" I ask. "What does it mean?"

"*Dedushka* means grandfather," she educates me with a proud puff of her chest. "Grandfather can't wait to meet you."

And just like that, the warmth fizzles out, replaced by a cold sense of dread.

*I am so fuckitty-fucked.*

# Chapter 25

*Victor*

**GRIGORI'S HUNCHED** across from us, thinking he's the big shot with his backup goons spread around. They're eyeing us like we're some Sunday school boys they can push over.

Big mistake.

Misha and Ari flank me, muscles tensed, ready to leap into action. We're not just big; we're a damn fortress, and these clowns are about to find out.

Vasiliev's crew plays it cautious, never bunching up their top dogs in one spot—clever, but not clever enough. Here I am, arms crossed, looking every bit the brute I am known to be. My fists itch for a fight, hidden but ready. I've got a rep that makes grown men piss their pants, and though they've got numbers, we've got the might.

"Listen up, Grigori..." I lean in, my gaze boring into him like a drill. My hand casually rests on the table, inches from the concealed gun underneath. "You and your merry band of fuckups better start singing a different tune. We're not here for pleasantries." I sit back, my eyes cold. "I'm here to give you a choice. Return what you stole, or brace for the storm."

Grigori's sneer stretches across his face like he's king of the world, his goons forming a half-moon barrier around us. The tension in the air is thick, like we're on the edge of a knife.

I see him shift uncomfortably in his chair.

"Fucking kidding me?" Grigori spits, his voice oozing contempt. "You three think you own us? Vasiliev rules these streets, Morozov, not your pathetic excuse of a family."

"The Morozovs don't fuck around," I sneer, my gaze sharp, cutting through the tension like a knife. "Six decades, our family's ruled these shit-stained streets. Our legacy's built on blood, iron, loyalty. Everyone and their mother know we've got the biggest, baddest army around."

I glance around, scanning Grigori's men with a mocking grin. "Ari here," I nod toward the giant by my side, "could take your pathetic crew down solo. No sweat."

Grigori's jaw clenches, a vein throbbing at his temple. He knows he's cornered, but he's not the type to go down without a fight.

"*Morozov*," he snarls, his voice rough like gravel, "you think you can just walk in here and dictate terms?"

My reply is a cold smile, one that doesn't reach my eyes. "I don't think, Grigori. I know."

He's a beast of a man, muscle-bound and battle-hardened, but in this moment, there's a flicker of uncertainty in his eyes. It's a subtle crack in his armor, but it's all I need.

Misha, standing like a silent ghost at my back, lets out a soft, derisive snort. Ari, the human equivalent of a war machine, stares at Grigori with a look that could curdle blood.

"Listen, I don't have time to waste with you cockroaches," I growl, irritation seething through my words. "You have until the end of this week to return the cargo," I say. Moving forward, I plant my hands on the table and loom over them. The muscles in my forearms flex as I dig my fingers into the polished wood, leaving no doubt that I mean business.

My mind keeps going back to Laura. I left her at home to come deal with these fucking morons. The thought of her there, alone with Ksenia, makes my jaw clench. Ksenia's not exactly known for her warm and fuzzy personality.

"Consider this your only warning." I shoot a glance at Misha, catching the slight nod he gives, a clear signal he's ready to unleash hell if needed. His fingers inch subtly toward the gun hidden under his jacket.

Grigori bristles, his men tensing up, hands inching toward concealed weapons. I can feel the violence in the air, a storm ready to break.

"Watch your mouth, Morozov," Grigori warns, his eyes flashing danger. "We've got enough firepower here to turn you and your boys into Swiss cheese."

I can't help but chuckle. "You think firepower's enough? You think guns make you strong?" I stand, towering over the table, imposing and unyielding. "It's not the weapons, Grigori. It's the will to use them. And believe me, we've got the will."

*I'd relish the thought of rearranging your face, but I'm not about to ruin my look with your blood today.*

Misha shifts, a barely perceptible movement, but enough to send a clear message to Grigori's men. Ari cracks his neck, an ominous sound in the tense silence.

Grigori's laugh is forced, a feeble attempt to regain some ground. "Big words, Morozov. But words won't save you."

I stand, towering over the table. "We'll be in touch, Grigori. Tell fucking Ivan Vasiliev to return what's ours or brace for hell. This is your only warning."

As we turn to leave the restaurant, I can feel Grigori's eyes burning into our backs.

Misha's right beside me, his voice low. "This is going to turn ugly."

I nod, feeling the inevitable clash brewing. "We'll hit them where it hurts. They want war, they'll get it."

"We've got the men ready, boss. Locked, loaded, and waiting for your word. This is more than a skirmish; it's a declaration. They won't know what hit them," Misha assures me.

"We strike fast, no mercy," I instruct Ari. "Ivan Vasiliev should pay for stealing from us."

*Morozovs never kneel, especially not before fucking Vasiliev or any other pretender.*

I glance at my watch. "*Blyad*. It's almost time." I spit out a curse. Laura's face flashes in my mind. "Let's go," I command. "It's time to introduce my wife-to-be to the family. She won't stand a chance with them by herself."

The car cuts through the New York night like a knife, the streets outside a blur of shadows and neon. Ari's eyes are glued to the road, but I can tell he's ready to turn this car into a battering ram if he spots any of Vasiliev's rats tailing us. Misha's got his hawk eyes going, too, scanning every alleyway and corner like he's expecting a bomb to go off.

"So, back to the house, huh?" Misha finally says, a smirk in his voice. I can almost hear the bastard grinning without looking.

I grunt, staring out the window. "Yeah, thrilled beyond words."

"It's tradition, boss," Ari chimes in, sounding like he's quoting from some ancient Bratva bible. "*Pakhan*'s gonna be pissin' himself with joy."

I scoff at that. "Screw tradition. He's just trying to put me in a box."

Misha lets out this low chuckle, thinking he's got it all figured out. "It's about the image, boss. Shows we're solid."

I watch him from the shadows in the back, his fingers dancing over the blade he's toying with—a clear sign he's mulling over something serious.

"You sure about this, boss?" He's not asking about the Vasiliev or the dinner.

It's about her—Laura.

*Everyone's* been on my case about her like I owe them an explanation.

"She's not just some girl," I finally spit out. "She's a debt being paid."

"Right, boss."

I send him a glare. "Watch it. Brother."

He smirks, unfazed. "You've been all about her since the day we tracked her down."

A warning look is all I give him. Misha's been in the trenches with me for a decade, the only guy I really trust, but he's still my underboss. He doesn't fear anyone, not even the *pakhan*. Honesty is his thing, and it's usually welcome—just not now.

"Look, like I say, she's practical."

Misha looks at me with a wink. "Right. Very practical. Tell me, was it also very *practical* to drag her to your suite?"

My stare could freeze hell over, but Misha, he's got the guts to meet it. He knows he can. He's seen the darkest corners of our world, owes his life to my old man. But his loyalty doesn't give him a free pass today.

I arch an eyebrow at him. "You spying on me now?"

"Just making sure you're not slipping, boss. With a girl like that, you never know. She could turn your world upside down."

I run a hand through my hair. "What pisses me off is you doubting my call."

He snorts. "Just watching your back, boss." Misha's smirk fades into something more serious as he turns his attention back to the road. "Your safety comes first."

I've always trusted Misha. Since we were just kids—me at five and him at seven—when my father introduced us and gave us toy guns to play with. We'd run around, pretending to be characters from "Jonny Quest," thinking we were on some big adventure, fighting bad guys and saving the day.

Those days are long gone, but the bond we built has never faded. Now, we're dealing with real dangers, not just make-believe. But it's like nothing's really changed between us. Misha's still got my back, just like he did when we were shooting at imaginary villains in the backyard. It's us against the world, just like it's always been.

The car moves smoother, the city sounds are a distant echo now. I can't help but think about Laura, how bringing her into this mess is a gamble.

"I'm not looking to get tied down, married, or chained to anyone. Laura's just here for a year, a straightforward business transaction, nothing more." I start to justify my actions, questioning why I even feel the need to.

Misha snorts. "Sure, boss."

I'm about to retort when he shifts the topic. "Speaking of which, I've got news on that piece of shit, Dave Jankowski."

I lean forward, interest spiked. "Where is the bastard?" I crack my knuckles.

Misha turns around from the front seat, angling in a bit so I catch every word clearly. "That rat's back, roaming around New York," he says. "And guess what? He's been lurking around Laura's apartment."

My brow furrows. "What the hell is he after now?"

Misha shrugs, his gaze hard. "We're not sure yet, boss. Seems like he's got more dirty secrets up his sleeve."

The thought of him near Laura sets off a storm inside me, raw and raging.

"If that *suka* so much as breathes in her direction, I want him six feet under. Clear?"

# Chapter 26

*Victor*

"WE'RE HERE boss." Ari announces, pulling the G-Class to a stop in front of the main house. My eyes crack open, catching the estate's green rush outside the window. Looks like I caught a few minutes of sleep without meaning to.

I grunt in response, checking my watch.

*Just in time.*

"Good luck, boss," Misha teases from the front seat, turning to throw me a smirk.

I shoot back a glare. "*Zakroy svoy rot*, Misha. Make sure everything's ready in twenty-four hours. Those Vasilievs won't hand over our shipment without a fight."

Misha chuckles. "Don't sweat it. We've got their location pinned down. Just finalizing the numbers."

I nod, the unease in my gut growing. The wedding's in two days, and there's no way I'm letting the Vasilievs mess with the Morozovs—not on my watch.

Stepping out of the SUV, the mansion looms, a fortress filled with memories, both good and bad. As the guards open the gates and doors, I can't help but feel the weight of what's coming.

The family's all inside, including Laura, my soon-to-be wife.

*Shit, why does that thought twist me up inside?*

Straightening my suit jacket, I stride toward the house.

Entering the dining room, the grandeur of the Morozov estate is on full display. The long table is set with fine china and crystal, the chandeliers casting a soft glow over everything. My father sits at the head of the table, his facial expression is relaxed and strangely—*cheerful.*

"Probably the meds," I murmur, a smirk tugging at my lips.

I haven't sat for a family dinner in years, always finding an excuse to skip. But not today.

"Sorry for the delay," I mutter, more out of formality than actual regret.

Ksenia smirks. "Fashionably late as always, Victor."

I ignore her jibe and slip into my seat beside our father.

Placing my hands on the grand, age-worn dining table that has seen generations of our family's gatherings, a server discreetly approaches, pouring a deep red wine into my glass with practiced elegance.

Taking a sip, my eyes skip over Dimitry, my brother-in-law, and pause on Yuri, my nephew. Yuri's different now. Last time I saw him, he was just a kid. Now he's tall, looks like he's been working out, and there's something about him that's just… off. He's not really looking at anyone, just kind of lost in his own world.

Around the table, cousins and their wives whom I barely recognize anymore give me those wary looks. Respect mixed with a bit of fear, like they're not sure if I'm going to toast to family or start a brawl.

Down the table, Dr. Petrov catches my eye, and we share a brief nod—an unspoken acknowledgment between us.

He's here for one reason: keeping an eye on the *Pakhan*, our headstrong patriarch.

I sweep the room, my eyes hunting for Laura among the faces.

*Where is she?*

My attention is pulled to those solid wooden doors across the room, waiting for someone to walk through them.

I force myself to look away, puzzled by my own actions.

*Why the hell am I even looking for her?*

I take a bigger gulp of my wine, trying to drown the irritation. Footsteps echo from the kitchen direction, stirring a brief hope.

*Blyad*. It's just the server with appetizers.

*Get a fucking grip,* I scold myself silently, my gaze returning to the table.

"Is everything going according to plan?" my father asks me, his voice steady but his eyes betraying a hint of frailty.

Ksenia cuts in before I can speak. "The wedding's all set for Saturday. Everything Is booked, from the church to the reception hall…" She pauses, her voice dropping to ensure I'm all ears for the bomb she's about to drop.

"Invitations went out to the families, and…" She trails off, her eyes locking onto mine, a smirk playing at the corners of her lips.

"Petrovas and Smirnovs ain't happy," she goes on, her smirk turning sharp. "Seems none of their daughters made the cut this time." Her tone's laced with a bitter satisfaction, a clear jab at me picking Laura over their high-bred stock.

Frustration bubbles up, and I take a swig of my wine, barely tasting it. My eyes flick to the appetizer in front of me—smoked salmon on toasted bruschetta garnished with a sprig of dill. Looks fancy, but my mind's elsewhere. I sneak another look at the door, hoping, then snap back as my father coughs.

"What about the shipments?" he probes, voice laced with concern over the fifteen million in arms we've got floating somewhere between here and Vasiliev's greedy fingers.

"Nothing to worry about, Papa," I assure him, my tone more confident than I feel. "It'll be settled. *Before* the wedding."

Ksenia chimes in, surprisingly on my side for once, "You don't need to worry about Bratva affairs tonight, Papa." Her eyes flicker to me; for once, I agree with my sister.

"Just focus on not keeling over during your surgery," I shoot a look at the doctor then back at my father.

His laughter booms across the table, startling a few of the distant cousins into spilling their drinks. "Cocky as ever," he retorts, eyes twinkling despite the weariness. "Remember, boy, you'll be in my shoes one day, old and nagging someone younger to take it easy on you."

I can't help but snort, leaning back in my chair. "By then, I'll have someone to boss around, too, won't I?"

He nods, a serious glint replacing the mirth. "That's why finding the right woman, one to bear heirs, is critical. You think I want our legacy to crumble?"

The atmosphere in the room subtly shifts. Some guests discreetly nod in agreement with my father's statement, avoiding direct eye contact. Meanwhile, Dimitry offers a muted smirk, partially concealing it behind his napkin. Yuri, on the other hand, remains engrossed in his phone, sipping his wine without any visible reaction, seemingly waiting for a message or call.

I meet my father's gaze squarely. "Legacy's one thing, but chaining myself to someone just for heirs? That's another ballgame."

Ksenia leans forward, taking a slow sip of her wine, leaving a bold red lipstick mark on the glass. "And yet, you've chosen someone… unconventional. Bold move, brother."

Her comment draws a round of murmured assents and a few disapproving clucks from the wives of my cousins, their entertainment clear. But a single sharp glance from me and their giggles die in their throats.

"Unconventional or not," I assert firmly, my tone leaving no room for debate, "she's got what's needed." I scan the table, my gaze a clear command for silence. "And if you're all done psychoanalyzing my choices, I'd like to eat in peace."

I tap my glass, annoyed that it's been empty too long. A server rushes over, refilling it as my gaze drifts to the two empty seats beside me. Eli's missing too.

Ksenia catches my glance, her smirk telling. "You are right, brother," she says, casually placing her napkin on her lap. "Tonight, we are going here to *welcome* Victor's new wife."

*Ah, there it is.* Ksenia giving me that look. Like she's already plotting ten ways to make Laura's night hell.

I knock back a bigger gulp of wine, its sharp tang mirroring my frustration. Then I hear Eli's voice, bright and excited, from the other side of the door. "She's finally here, everyone!"

The door creaks open.

My heart stops, my breath catches, and there, in that sliver of a moment, everything changes.

I gasp at the sight…

# Chapter 27

*Victor*

**EVERY HEAD** in the room turns.

My cousins let out dry coughs, their wives glaring at them for their obvious reactions as Laura steps into the room hand in hand with Eli.

For a moment, it's as if everything slows down.

There she is.

She's fucking stunning, draped in a flowing beige chiffon dress that accentuates her every movement, her skin glowing in the soft light.

I can't help it—my skin prickles with something akin to pure desire as I watch her approach. Laura's self-assured steps falter just slightly, her eyes meeting mine across the room.

I stand up, almost robotic as I pull out her chair.

*Weird. I'm acting like she's got me under some damn spell.*

The scent of jasmine and vanilla hits me like a punch to my cock. It's impossible to ignore the throbbing between my legs as I inhale her intoxicating aroma.

*Goddamn, she makes me horny as fuck.*

I let my hand glide over her shoulder, a raw, intimate gesture. "You're late," I say bluntly.

Her body stiffens, and she inhales sharply. I can tell she's biting back some snarky response.

"*Late?* Maybe because no sane person speeds to their own kidnapper," she whispers fiercely.

Giving her a smug smile, I lean toward her, close enough to catch that intoxicating mix of jasmine and vanilla again.

"Sit," I growl, eyes locked on hers, observing her closely.

Her dress is decent enough, but it hugs tight against her plump tits, drawing my gaze downward. Her skin is flawless. Knowing that I will soon have the privilege of unwrapping her and exploring every inch of her body makes my groin tweak.

"I'm not your pet." Her cheeks flush, but her chin lifts, defiant. "What's going on here?" she breathes, her gaze sweeping quickly across the table.

Grudgingly, I drag my eyes back up to her face.

"Tradition. Family meets before the wedding."

Laura halts halfway to sitting. Her gaze on me, wild. She gulps, her throat working hard over words she can't seem to let out.

Right then, a server slides in, breaking the ice without even knowing it. "Wine, ma'am?" he offers, oblivious to the standoff.

Her eyes flicker to him, then around the room, suddenly clocking the audience for this little drama, including the old man at the end of the table—the *pakhan*, giving her the once-over.

"No, no…thanks," she mutters to the server, finally taking the seat next to me, a reluctant surrender. "Water will do, please."

Papa leans forward, his eyes softening as they meet Laura's.

*What the hell?*

This is new to me.

Seeing him like this, with that soft look in his eyes and an easy smile on his lips, throws me off. He's always been the epitome of a strict and no-nonsense father, never showing any sign of weakness or vulnerability. I can't help but wonder when he started going soft.

"Hello, I am Andrey, Andrey Morozov," he introduces himself. "Victor's father."

Laura's body stiffens next to me, her hands squeezing the napkin on her lap as if it's my neck.

I smirk.

*That's my girl.*

Truth is, anyone else would be a mess, probably scared shitless. But here she is, standing strong, barely letting the fear show. It's a shock how well she's handling this madness.

I should be parading her around, doing the whole meet-and-greet. But honestly? I couldn't give a damn. These so-called cousins, they're just here for show. Been leeching off my father's success forever, twisting our family's wins into their own gains without lifting a finger.

"Hello," Laura replies, her voice little more than a whisper. "I-I'm Laura," she stammers, her eyes darting around as if looking for an escape route.

The whole table goes quiet, like someone farted in church. I mean, no one saw this coming.

I guess no one expected the *pakhan* to react this way to a girl not from the mafia or business blood tie. Now I know why Ksenia warned Laura not to tell anyone about our arrangement. The whole goal here is to get this stubborn old man to consent to his surgery.

"I'm… I… guess… I'm… Victor's…"

Before Laura gets more tangled in her words, Eli, with all the honesty a kid can muster, cuts in.

"She's Victor's bride, *dedushka*!"

A few chuckles ripple through the room, more polite than genuine. My father's laughter breaks through, hearty and loud.

"Well, Eli, thank you for spelling it out for everyone."

Ksenia remains quiet, gulping down her wine with dark eyes. I can almost read her thoughts: she's betting Laura won't last a day here—let alone a year—once she gets a real taste of our life.

I watch as Laura's cheeks flush a deep crimson as she chugs her glass of water. She tries to force a smile that barely conceals her embarrassment and discomfort.

I signal to the server to refill her glass and then quickly reach for her hand. I give it a small squeeze, silently communicating for her to stay calm. As I release her hand, I place my hands back on the table and cut into a slice of salmon, taking a bite and savoring the flavor.

"So, Laura," my father continues, eager to know more, "how did you two meet?"

Laura turns, and when our eyes meet, a jolt of electricity shoots through me.

Laura's eyes dart between me and Papa, then lock onto mine. Her expression is a comically exaggerated mix of fear and panic, silently begging me for help. I can't hold back a silent chuckle at her ridiculous face, trying to hide the absurdity of the situation from the old man who sits clueless in his chair. Laura looks like a trapped animal, pleading with me through her wide eyes. I give her a subtle wink, reassuring her that I've got this under control.

She glances back at Papa. "We... uh... It was at the club," she stammers out while I confidently state: "At her bookstore."

Quickly jerking her head around, staring at me intently, her lips press together. It takes everything in me not to burst out laughing at her expression.

This little interaction might just be the highlight of my day.

One eyebrow arched in amusement, Papa asks, "So, it's the club? Or the bookstore?" His gaze shifts between me and Laura.

Taking another sip of my wine, I feel it burn a trail of heat down my throat.

I lean back and start to spin a tale. "I was hunting down a debt owed to us when I stumbled into her dingy bookstore," I say, bending the truth just a bit. "Then, she ended up at my club." I continue, stealing a glance at Laura.

Out of the corner of my eye, I see her nervously take a sip of water. I press on with the story. "That's where she fell for me, like a fool," I say, a smirk playing on my lips. I catch Laura trying hard not to roll her eyes at me, a vein in her neck standing out as she restrains herself.

"So, I proposed, and she said yes." I struggle to hold back my laughter when she nearly chokes on her water but manages to catch herself just in time. She quickly dabs at her mouth with a napkin and shoots daggers at me with her eyes.

"And just like that," I declare, the smirk fully formed now, "we're getting married in three days."

I look over at Eli, noticing her gaze fixed on me, her eyes wide with fascination. She's hanging onto every word, thinking this is some kind of epic romance. I give her a playful wink, and she responds with a bright, innocent giggle.

"Sure you did," Papa scoffs, shaking his head in disbelief at my brief summary of our "love story." He then shifts his focus to my soon-to-be wife, who seems to be wishing for the floor to swallow her up.

Turning his attention fully toward her, he asks, "So, you own a bookstore?"

"I assure you, Papa, she will fit right in with our family," I cut him off, looking for a way to switch gears. "How about we start with dinner?" I pivot to Eli.

"YES!" Eli's excitement cuts through the tension. She rubs her belly, lips pressed in anticipation. "I'm starving!"

"Indeed, the kitchen is ready to impress, especially for you, Papa," Ksenia adds, smoothing over any remaining awkwardness.

Our father exhales a tired sign and gives a nod of approval, and I catch a server's eye, nodding to bring in the feast.

A knot twists in my gut as I catch sight of the old man, so fragile after the stroke. It's like the backbone of our family is bending, about to snap. He's got to get back on his feet, and soon.

*Derr'mo*, it's on me now. Can't let anyone see the worry, the crack in our armor. It's bigger than just him; it's about keeping the empire from smelling fear.

Right then, my phone vibrates. I pull the device out of my suit jacket, and a message from Misha flashes on the screen: "Eyes on the prize at Dockside Warehouse. The goods are there."

*Misha's reliable, as always.*

Just as I'm about to stash the phone away, another message blinks into view:

"We lost track of Dave Jankowski."

# Chapter 28

*Laura*

**THE CLOCK** on the wall chimes nine. Its sound is rich, like everything else here.

Two hours in, I'm frozen in place, like a rag doll set out for show.

Finally, our twelfth dish makes its grand entrance, a delicate dessert that looks more like art than food.

The Michelin Star chef himself emerges from the kitchen. This culinary wizard, with sleeves rolled up over tattooed arms and stubble shadowing his jaw, looks like he's just won a battle as he sets down a plate of tiny, almost laughable pastries.

"Our finale," he announces, "a deconstructed tiramisu, paired with a raspberry coulis and a quenelle of white chocolate mousse. And for our young miss," the chef declares, "we've specially prepared an alcohol-free Chocolate Degustation. Please, enjoy."

I bite back a laugh, puzzled by the tiny portions.

*Mental note: Rich folks have weird standards for what counts as food.*

In my head, I'm calculating if I've eaten enough to qualify as a full meal by any standard. Spoiler: I haven't. The thought crosses my mind that anyone normal would find this dining experience utterly ridiculous. Twelve courses, and I'm still fantasizing about a late-night burger run.

I scowl, realizing a late-night burger run is off the table. I'm trapped here; no two ways about it. I did all this, walked straight into danger, now putting Ser and her family in danger because of me.

Sitting here, surrounded by the Morozov Bratva clan, I never thought I'd be breaking bread—or tiny, artistic twelve-course meals—with gangsters.

*Ser would've penned an entire novel by now, something about a vampire preparing for a wedding feast where the bride unknowingly stars as the main dish.*

Thinking about Ser squeezes my heart tight, sparking a silent wish to see her again.

I let out a covert sigh, messing with the cutlery like it's a puzzle.

I feel them around me; the table's under a spotlight of glares, especially from the far end where a brunette and a dark-haired woman sit, their thick makeup hiding any genuine emotion. The weight of their stares makes my skin prickle.

They catch my eye, whispering something to each other before erupting into fake laughter.

"Yeah, thrilled to be here too, ladies," I silently jeer. Victor skips the introductions, diving straight into the meal like it's just another Sunday brunch.

*But then, what's the point? We're only pretending. I'm not his real bride-to-be.*

I dodge the icy stares with a swift glance, my eyes quickly shifting away from the mean girls.

Among them, a man catches my attention—quiet, his gaze fixed ahead, not with the chill of a hitman, but with a blend of sorrow and strength.

I take a nervous sip of water and follow his gaze to the head of the table, to Andrey Morozov himself. He's talking to Victor, both of them holding themselves like they own the world.

Clearly, Victor inherited his stunning looks from his father.

Despite his years, Andrey exudes an air of command that's hard to ignore, his suit crisp, his bearing one of innate leadership. His whole vibe screams "battle-hardened," but it's the unexpected softness in his eyes tonight that throws me.

My eyes wander, settling on Victor. He's undeniably handsome, features cut sharp and unmistakably masculine.

*Holy smokes! Is that jawline chiseled out of marble, or what? Looks like it could cut glass.*

The way it clenches when he's focused. Heat crawls up my cheeks, uninvited.

Then, abruptly, he turns, our eyes lock, and I'm caught.

*Fuck, fuck, shit.*

Panic flutters in my chest, and I blink rapidly, turning away as my fingers find refuge in twisting a lock of my hair

Thank God Eli's excitement rescues me from being busted for ogling Victor. "Look at this, Laura!" Her wonder's infectious. Her eyes light up like it's Christmas, almost bouncing in her seat. "Wow, they're so pretty!" she bursts out when the server places the plate before her.

I lean toward her, forcing a smile. "They really are, aren't they?"

It's the least I can do, giving her a moment in this madness. My mind's racing, still struggling to make sense of it all.

As I lift my gaze, it clashes with Ksenia's. That dead stare of hers hits me again before she shifts her attention to the young man sitting opposite her.

He's striking, resembling a model straight off a runway with his sad, dark gray eyes. He acknowledges Ksenia with a subtle nod, then immerses himself back in his phone.

Seriously, is there a factory churning out these ridiculously handsome men around here?

I can't help but wonder about his identity, noticing he carries the same frosty aura as Ksenia.

*Seriously? Laur?*

This is *not* the right time or place for eyeing men like I'm flipping through a catalog. Did I not remember that in just three days, I'm about to tie the knot with a Russian mafia boss?

And Dad... How on Earth do I break this to him, or to anybody, for that matter?

I find my fingers nervously playing with the fork, aimlessly tracing the outlines of a tiny, leftover flower garnish from the last course, almost like I'm trying to dissect its secrets.

"Ma'am," a server gently cuts through my daze, skillfully sliding a new plate in front of me while whisking the old one away. "Your dessert," he announces.

"Thanks," I grunt to the server as he sets down what's supposed to be the grand finale of a meal.

My eyes can't help but flick over to Victor. He's dabbing his mouth with a napkin. He has his sleeves rolled up to his forearms; those ridiculous, stupid large arms with veins standing out as if carved from stone, annoyingly, turn on a feeling I can't shake.

My throat suddenly feels dry, and without thinking, I swallow hard, trying to ease the tightness between my legs. My body is reacting without my control.

*Okay, it's clear now—I've totally lost it. How am I getting these... these tingles from a guy who's practically kidnapped and forced me into a marriage I never asked for?*

A hushed sigh slips out as I tackle the miniature dessert with a fork that feels like it's made for ants.

I nudge that tiny dessert into my mouth, and— *Holymotherofgod*, my tongue just had an orgasm!

"Mmmm..." I groan, licking my lips to savor the lingering taste of tiramisu. One bite, and it's all gone.

"That was a quick trip to heaven," I murmur, sliding the fork out of my mouth.

I raise my eyes, and there he is, watching.

His stare travels from my lips up to my eyes. Hard, deep, and like a predator.

A sultry heat weaves through my bloodstream. I'm melting quicker than ice cream on a hot day.

*Damnit, Laur, get it together.*

I break his stare. "Ex-excuse me, restroom ... break," I manage to stammer out as I push my chair back. My body is on fire, and all I can think about is getting away from him.

"Let me walk you there," Victor says, standing tall, quieting the entire room.

"I can find it myself," I whisper back, attempting to maintain some distance between us. But who am I kidding? Victor is going to get what he wants.

Without hesitation, he extends his hand, and I know it's not a request. It's a demand.

Looking up at his big, strong body, my face flushes hot, and my heart does a little tap dance. A sudden wave of desire hits me like a fiery burrito from last night's Taco Tuesday.

*Goddamnit, Laur.*

Cursing under my breath, I clench my jaw as I refuse to hand over my hand. But he just smirks and challenges me with a look. "You'll get lost on your own," he teases.

Before I can object again, I'm stopped short. "Eh-hmm," an awkward interruption from Andrey Morozov makes me shift my gaze, my lips pressing together tightly. The Morozovs' eyes are on us, silent and assessing, except for Eli, whose yawn breaks the tension momentarily. I divert my gaze, feeling out of place.

I bite my lip down, my eyes flicking elsewhere, knowing I'd really rather be anywhere but here. With a reluctant sigh, I give in, placing my hand in his. His grip is surprisingly comforting, a solid presence amidst my inner chaos.

Yet, the moment is fleeting. Victor's hand encases mine, a smirk touching his lips as he whispers close, "There's my good girl."

"I'm nobody's '*good girl,*'" I retort softly.

"Excuse us," Victor announces to the room, leading me away with a confidence that draws every eye.

I hear my heels gently clicking onto the marble floor as Victor leads me out of the dining hall, our bodies brushing against each other with every step. I can feel the tension and desire building.

But I know better than to give in. This may be just another one of Victor's manipulative tactics, using me to appear even more powerful and desirable.

*Jerk.*

I let him lead me toward a corridor, its walls mirrored from end to end. Catching our reflection, I barely recognize myself beside him. The old Laura, in casual wear and untamed hair, is nowhere to be seen. Instead, there stands a woman who looks like she has it all together—poised, polished, and paired with a man who could be straight out of a magazine.

For a second, the image captivates me.

For a second, I look like someone with a perfect life.

I clench my jaw, reminding myself.

*This isn't my life. It never will be.*

No matter how tempting the illusion may be.

# Chapter 29

*Laura*

"WHERE'S THE bathroom?" I demand, trying to break the silence that's settled between us.

Victor gives me a look, amusement flickering in his eyes. "Thinking of making a run for it? It's a long way to the nearest Starbucks, just so you know."

I snort. "Please! Like I could escape. I'd probably get lost in your closet."

He shoots me a roguish smirk, the kind that spells trouble and has temptation written all over it, then steers us both away from the dining hall, guiding me deeper into the mansion's maze-like corridors.

Walking through this mansion feels like trekking across a small country, except with more chandeliers and less fresh air. We stroll past guards who nod like they're part of the royal guard and maids with smiles so fixed, I wonder if they're superglued on.

The place is so stuffed with luxury it's like breathing in dollar bills—suffocating and slightly absurd. The endless parade of rooms and corridors starts to blend together into one big, lavish blur.

Victor glances at me, a flicker of knowing in his eyes.

"You don't need the bathroom," he says, his grip on my hand firm yet not unkind. We're close, our bodies nearly touching as we walk.

"Maybe I do," I say, frustrated. I'm making a valiant attempt to yank my hand back, but let's face it, in this tug-of-war, I'm as likely to win as a Chihuahua in a heavyweight boxing match. My hand in his feels like a peanut tucked in the palm of a giant—Luka's hands could probably double as catchers' mitts without anyone batting an eye.

"Let go of me."

"Not happening."

Fine, I quit. Picking battles wisely is apparently a skill I need to sharpen, especially around him.

"You know, a few signs wouldn't hurt. I've officially lost my breadcrumbs back to the dining hall."

He aims a quick glance at me. "You'll learn your way around soon enough. You have a year to get used to this place," Victor says with that chilly detachment of his.

"Oh, joy. A whole year to become a human GPS of the Morozov Manor. Can't wait," I retort.

His lips twitch; a hint of a smile, maybe? Or a prelude to a snarl. With Victor, it's hard to tell. "Enthusiasm. I like that," he deadpans, leading me down another corridor that looks like all the others—gold, gaudy, and grossly grand.

I bite my lip, pondering over the contract, the wedding, the entire bizarre scenario I've found myself in. Questions swirl in my head like a particularly annoying swarm of bees, but fear clamps down on my tongue. What does one ask a mafia lord about a contract that's more a leash than a legal document?

"So, about this wedding…" I begin, but my voice trails off. The words feel like boulders, too heavy to haul into the open.

Victor's gaze flickers to me, and for a moment, I see the shift—from the lord of the manor to the predator assessing its prey. It's a look that says I'm playing a game whose rules I don't quite understand.

"What about it?" he prompts. As he says this, his grip on my hand tightens, almost like he's worried I'll bolt at the first chance.

"Should I expect doves, or is that too 'subtle' for the Morozov flair?"

He hesitates for a moment, considering. "Actually, we lean toward dragons, but it turns out they don't follow directions well," he jokes, guiding me through yet another lavish hallway.

"Didn't realize you had a sense of humor," I remark, keeping my tone light despite the swirling questions about the contract, the wedding, and what my future holds in this gilded cage.

Two maids approach and Victor's demeanor shifts to his usual jerk self. He doesn't smile or make eye contact.

We turn a corner, and the corridor narrows. The decorations here are sparse, a stark contrast to the lavishness we've left behind. The air grows cooler, the ambiance shifting. My curiosity is piqued despite my apprehension.

"Seriously, where are we going?"

Victor pauses before a door that seems ripped from a history book, all aged wood and iron. He lets go of my hand, pushing the door open. No eerie creak follows, just a silent swing that reveals a room unlike any other in the mansion.

"Victor, this doesn't look like any bathroom I've ever seen," I remark as I step into the room.

The walls are lined with family photos in black and white, their edges yellowed with age, the faces stoic. I can't help but wander closer, drawn to the dates marking monumental moments—World War I, World War II.

I turn, taking in every detail, and I notice more than just photographs. Every item in the room is thoughtfully arranged.

There's a display of antiques: a vase with intricate patterns, a statue of a Chinese horse that looks like it belongs in a museum, and newspaper cuttings framed on the wall, telling stories of past glories and tragedies.

My steps slow as I approach a massive wall filled with faces from another era, their expressions captured in grayscale. My eyes scan the dates, each one a gateway to a story long concluded.

"Are these your ancestors?" I ask, unable to hide the awe in my voice. My jaw slackens as the magnitude of history before me sinks in. This room isn't just utilitarian; it's also a personal museum, showing off the Morozov Bratva's legendary history that goes way back.

Victor is behind me, watching, a hint of pride flickering in his eyes.

"Every family has its guardians of history."

"But… why are you… showing these to me?" Whipping around, I shoot him a questioning look.

There's a glint of mischief in his eyes. "Patience, little firecracker."

It's like my heart's caught in a high-speed chase as I watch him lock the door with purposeful clicks.

He turns and starts walking toward me; his intense stare travels up and down my body, leaving a trail of heat in its wake.

I can't tear my gaze away from his; shock courses through me as my body betrays me, my nipples hardening into tight peaks. A surge of intense heat ignites between my thighs, causing me to gasp for air.

I press my lips together, mustering every ounce of fake confidence I have.

"Planning to lock me up in some secret chamber for a year?" The question flies out before I can stop it, suddenly feeling way too real.

Inside, I'm practically screaming. A million and one thoughts ricochet through my mind.

Victor just strides closer, a predator in a suit. Before I know it, he's in my personal space.

I instinctively step back until—thud.

My head nearly collides with the wall, but his hand is there, cushioning the blow. Great, now he's literally the only thing standing between me and a concussion.

He's so close I can count the threads in his suit.

"Why? Do you *want* to get locked up in a secret chamber?"

My eyes narrow. "Asshole," I snap back.

Victor's eyebrows raise. "Let me remind you, asking too many questions isn't exactly healthy around here."

I'm breathing heavily, staring into those goddamn captivating, wild gray eyes.

"You don't scare me," I bluff, quickly dropping my gaze to avoid those intense eyes, landing on his chest instead. Big mistake. His chest looks like it's straight out of an action hero's wardrobe, all muscle and no fluff.

"Back off, or I swear—

Victor laughs, low and husky. "Warnings from you sound more like invitations."

Pushing against what feels like a marble statue, I try to regain some personal space.

To my utter shock, he takes a step back, his smirk turning into a twisted grin. "Remember that fire when we fuck. Let's see just how explosive you can be, little firecracker."

*What the hell did he just say?!*

My blood runs cold at the suggestion, and I open my mouth to protest, but his hand shoots up toward my face.

*Great, now he's going to silence me the old-fashioned way.*

I flinch and brace myself to scream, but… instead, his fingers brush past my ear, and there's this beep sound. Like magic, the wall behind me shifts, and I'm falling backward, only to be yanked back into his arms.

He's got me now, close enough that I can feel the heat radiating off him, and all I can think is how absurdly good he smells—like sin and something spicy, a scent that makes me want to forget why I was mad in the first place.

Victor steadies me with a firm grip.

"Let's go," he says, his voice steady. I catch his gaze, then turn around.

"What the…?" I stumble over my words.

# Chapter 30

*Laura*

"**WELL SLAP** me sideways," I blurt out, my eyes darting between Victor and the entrance to this hidden passage to the unknown.

I'm trying not to let my jaw hit the floor because the wall, along with its parade of antiques and family history, just vanishes like a magic trick.

"You actually have a secret chamber down there?" My voice sounds as brave as a kitten in a dog park. I glance down at the passage that's suddenly revealed, its tiles so intricately detailed and historic, they'd put the finest gallery to shame.

"Come with me," Victor commands, his hand a steady presence on my back, guiding me forward as my body trembles with a cocktail of emotions. My mind's racing with wild, not entirely appropriate fantasies about what might lie beneath us.

*This can't be real, can it? What if there's a secret BDSM lair?*

As we step down, Victor's hand clasps mine, providing some warmth in the chilly air surrounding us like a cloak. Suddenly, a high-tech sensor goes off, and the door—excuse me, *wall*—seals us inside. The loud click makes me shiver, along with the cold draft coming from somewhere.

My eyes are wide, every sense on high alert. "Victor, you need to tell me where we're going," I demand.

Rooted to the spot, I make it clear—I'm not taking another step until he gives me an answer.

"My father built this chamber for my mother," he reveals, his voice softening with nostalgia and sorrow. As he talks, he nudges me forward, guiding me down the steps with him.

"Your mother?" I blurt out, trying to connect the pieces. There was no older woman beside Andrey at the family dinner tonight.

*Holy fuck, did his dad really lock his mom in a secret underground chamber?*

Nervously, I nibble at my lip, eyeing him. My imagination kicks into overdrive, spinning out all kinds of dark scenarios.

He chuckles. "You've got it wrong," he says, his gaze fixed ahead as we keep moving down. The dim light throws his face into shadow, showing a hint of something sad I hadn't seen in him till now.

*And now he can read minds. Great.*

"She's dead," he states simply, a flicker of vulnerability in his voice that he quickly smothers.

I feel a twinge of unexpected empathy.

My curiosity about her death, appearance, it all bubbles up, but I push it down.

*Not the right time, Laur.*

"I'm sorry," I offer softly, squeezing his hand in mine. "Lost my mom young too."

We stare at each other for a moment, a glimpse of something on his face—a flicker of shared understanding, maybe—before he masks it with that familiar stoic veneer.

"It happens." He shrugs, his voice flat as we make our way down the cold stairs. "People die."

"Achoo!" The sneeze rips through the silence, bouncing off the walls.

*Great, just what I need at this time. A bloody sneeze.*

Embarrassed, I blush. Great timing, really, showing I'm not all tough.

His mouth quirks up on one side, and he drops his jacket on me. It's warm. I try to keep my guard up, but it's hard with his coat around me.

I push away the soft thoughts, trying to remember we're in a mess, not a date.

"So, are you ever going to tell me where we're heading?" I shoot him a side glance, trying to muster a bit more boldness in my voice.

Before Victor can respond, he comes to a stop. I quickly turn my attention forward. An archway looms into view, reminiscent of a Moroccan palace, its tiles a riotous explosion of bohemian hues.

I blink rapidly, my mind racing to process the visual feast before my eyes.

"Holy—" I manage to choke out. This isn't just a chamber; it's Aladdin's cave on steroids.

I'm standing here, totally gobsmacked.

Jewelry—more jewelry than I've seen in my life—spills from every shelf. Sapphires, rubies, emeralds, diamonds gleaming like stars plucked from the sky. Even the watches look like they could fund a small country.

Victor could've told me we were crashing the treasure room of some ancient royalty, and I'd nod along. The place is dripping in so much bling it's like Scrooge McDuck decided to diversify into jewelry.

My idea of wealth is a fully stamped coffee loyalty card. This? This is another universe.

I can't help but think that my own jewelry collection is pretty much a set of pearls from Mom and… Oh yeah, a gold wedding band from my fake ex-husband.

"Hold on," he commands, his voice a low growl that prickles my skin.

Frozen in place, I watch Victor stride off, swiftly punching in a sequence that hushes the shrill alarms. "They belonged to my mother," he murmurs, a rare softness seeping into his tone. "Papa… He…" Victor begins, and right away, there's a slight shift in him.

He rakes his fingers through his hair and surveys the room with a swift look, his gaze darting from corner to corner as if searching for something unseen. It feels like he's about to share something he's not used to discussing.

It pulls me in, even though every logical part of me screams to run from anything tied to the Morozov Bratva.

We lock eyes, and something shifts.

His gray eyes, normally hard and distant, warm up a bit. He steps in, not like he's marching to battle, but like he wants to actually talk. Head tilted, he looks more human, less ice. Weird how there's suddenly this vibe between us.

"Papa liked to shower her with gifts, but she hardly wore them," he reveals, managing a brief, soft smile as he looks at the collection. For a moment, he appears more human, less the mafia jerk I was dragged here to marry.

"But… why? What…?"

He stops in front of me.

I have to tilt my head up just to meet his eyes. My lips are shivering, and it's not from the cold or fear but from the undeniable, crazy desire zapping between us, strong enough to rival any fictional tale I've scoffed at before. Is this the universe's way of saying "never say never?"

"Choose something for our wedding." His words snap me back to reality, and he gives me this nod.

I shoot him a wide-eyed stare, totally blindsided by his offer.

"Anything?" I squeak out.

"Yes,"

*Hold on, Laur.*

This has got to be a trap. He's probably got cameras ready to catch me pocketing a diamond the size of a golf ball.

My jaw clenches as I struggle to control my emotions. "I… I don't want it," I choke out.

But then my eyes are drawn to something, something that catches the light and glitters like shards of glass. My gaze locks onto the necklace hanging by the mirror—elegant curves and shimmering silver making everything around it pale in comparison. And there, dangling from a delicate chain is a teardrop-shaped diamond that seems to hold me captive. It's not just the size or sparkle that captivates me, but the sheer effortless beauty of it all—simple yet mesmerizing.

"I don't need any of this," I say, firm despite the teardrop necklace catching my eye. I force my attention back to Victor, serious.

His eyebrows shoot up like he's genuinely surprised. "Interesting. Why?"

He steps closer, his presence commanding. Instinctively, I take a half-step back, not ready to bridge the gap just yet.

"Most women would kill to have any piece of this beauty."

"Well, I'm *not* most women," I fire back, my hands finding their way to my hips in defiance.

"You'll look bare without jewelry at our wedding," he observes coolly. As if we're debating if the Earth is round or flat instead of this forced marriage.

"Our... wedding?" A mocking laugh escapes me. "Bare or not, I didn't *choose* this."

When he doesn't answer, irritation flares up inside me like a brushfire.

"You forced me into this marriage, remember?" My eyebrows knit together in a fierce glare.

"You signed the contract willingly," he counters, picking up a large green emerald and brushing off the invisible dust before he puts it back into a glass casing.

"Oh, right, because threatening my best friend is just your twisted version of courtship," I snap, my arms crossed tightly.

He moves in, and suddenly I'm hit with his scent—like danger had a one-night stand with a men's cologne ad. It's so overtly masculine that my ovaries are doing somersaults.

"Yes, I did," he admits without a hint of regret. "And I'm *not* sorry."

Right when I'm ready to explode, he drops this bombshell on me.

"I need you to marry me so Papa can get his surgery," he admits, brushing away a strand of hair falling in my face with a surprising gentleness.

"Excuse me, what now?" The fight in me starts to fizzle out, confusion taking over.

He hesitates, a rare break in his usually unflappable demeanor. "The old man had a stroke," he finally says, his voice rough with barely contained emotion. "Stubborn bastard won't get the help he needs unless I'm tied down."

I scoff, shaking my head.

It's a twisted kind of logic that makes my head spin. From threatening my friend to a forced marriage with a somewhat noble intent, it's a lot to process.

"But... why would someone like you not have options?" I push, my voice barely hiding the twinge of... is that jealousy? "Plenty of women would kill for your attention."

Quietly, he moves toward the display case, his back to me, and I can't help but watch the confident, assured way he holds himself.

"I don't know about killing. But you're right; there's no shortage of women throwing themselves at me," he says, turning back to me with the necklace in hand, his confidence as palpable as the chilled air between us. "But marrying any of them? Having little Victors running around? No, thank you. I'd rather jump out of a plane without a parachute."

I can't help but snort at the image of mini-Victors terrorizing the world. "So, what? You're just going to use me as a baby-making machine to appease your father?"

He chuckles, a deep, rumbling sound that sends shivers over my skin. "Tempting, but no. I have other plans for you, little firecracker."

I raise an eyebrow, trying to ignore the way my pulse quickens at his words. "Plans? What, like being your arm candy and smiling prettily for the cameras?"

He steps closer, his eyes glinting with something dark and dangerous. "Oh, you'll be doing a lot more than just smiling, Laura. Trust me on that."

I see the hunger in his eyes, the raw desire that threatens to consume us both. And despite every instinct telling me to run, to fight, I find myself leaning into his touch, craving more.

I swallow hard, my mouth suddenly dry.

"We need each other," he says, closing the distance between us.

He gently turns me around to face the mirror. His broad frame overshadows mine, our eyes clashing in the mirror's reflection.

The way he dubs me "little firecracker"—it's a mix of annoyance and allure. When he lifts his hand, the barely-there brush of his knuckles at my neck ignites a rush between my legs.

Seeing our reflection together, his proximity isn't just disarming—it's charged. As he loops the necklace around me, his fingertips graze my skin, then looks straight into my eyes.

"You're the perfect choice," he murmurs as the clasp clicks shut.

I clamp down on my lip, looking at him. A tingling warmth spreads from my heart to my veins.

"And this," he murmurs, his breath warm against my ear as he secures the teardrop earrings, "is just for a year. Then you're free—freedom and financial woes, all solved."

And there it is, the crux of it all.

He's standing there, telling me he's as trapped by this situation as I am—we're both prisoners of this forced marriage.

Victor looks from my eyes to the necklace and takes a deep breath.

"My mother's favorite," he says quietly, almost reverently. "She called it 'tears of a princess.'"

I reach out, fingers grazing the diamond. It's not screaming for attention, just elegantly lying there, shining against my skin. The light catches it just right, showing off its masterful cut—quiet but undeniable quality.

Now I'm wondering about Victor's mother, the woman who wore this before me. A *Pakhan*'s wife—was she pushed into marriage like I am? What was she like? How did she end up… dead?

"You…" Victor pauses, his Adam's apple bobbing, "look beautiful."

"Thanks…" I mutter, feeling a blush heat my cheeks, eyes darting away.

Victor takes a few steps back and heads toward a dark drawer on the other side of the room. I hear him open it, then close it. He turns back to face me, hesitates for a moment, then walks back to where I am. He's standing close to me now, close enough for me to see the flicker of uncertainty in his eyes. Without saying a word, he opens the box in his hands.

I hold my breath as I wait to see what's inside… I mean, I *know* what's inside.

Victor steps over, standing close to me, and there it is, the most stunning ring I've ever seen.

"Oh, my God." My eyes widen, not just from the sheer beauty of it but from the realization of what this represents.

"This was hers, too," he murmurs, his voice low.

I'm frozen, caught in the gravity of the moment, the ring sparkling as if it contains a piece of the night sky itself.

"Victor, I…" My voice trails off, words failing me.

*Oh God, this is the biggest rock I've ever seen.*

He steps closer, his hand reaching for mine. His touch is gentle, almost hesitant, as if he's giving me the chance to pull away. But I don't.

Instead, I let him take my hand and slide the ring on my finger. The pink diamond lights up the room, a dazzling display of wealth and power. But as it settles, the weight of it becomes apparent, both physically and metaphorically.

This ring, this moment, it's not a promise of love or devotion. It's a shackle, a gilded cage meant to bind me to him, to his world.

And as I stare at the glittering stone, I can't shake the feeling that I've just made a deal with the devil himself. A deal that will cost me more than I ever could have imagined.

The ring fits perfectly, like it was made just for me. But perfection, I'm learning, comes at a price.

And I'm not sure I'm ready to pay it.

# Chapter 31

*Victor*

**JUST A** few hours ago, I slid my mother's ring on Laura's finger.

Fuck, my balls tighten thinking of her soft skin, her intoxicating scent. I know what she wants, what her body craves. I can see it in the way she looks at me, the way she shivers under my touch.

I wish I could've taken her right there, bent her over the table, and fucked her until she screamed my name. I want to see her come undone, want to feel her tight heat clenching around my cock as she comes over and over again.

But there's no time for that. I had to send her back to our room, had to rush off to handle this operation tonight.

I have business to take care of, a score to settle.

I glance at my watch impatiently.

Only two more fucking hours of this bullshit left.

All I can think about is getting back to Laura. I need to bury myself inside that perfect pussy; need to make her mine in every way that matters. I want to hear her moan my name, want to feel her nails digging into my back as she begs me not to stop.

I can almost taste her, can almost feel the heat of her skin against mine. It's driving me crazy, this need, this hunger that only she can satisfy.

When I get back, I'm going to take my time with her. I'm going to worship every inch of that stunning body, going to tease her until she's a trembling, desperate mess. And then I'm going to make her come so hard she forgets her own name.

I won't stop until she's completely wrecked, until she's ruined for anyone else. I'll make her mine, body and soul, until there's no doubt in her mind that she belongs to me and me alone.

I adjust myself discreetly, my cock throbbing at the thought of having her all to myself, no interruptions, no distractions.

Just need to crush this prick Ivan first for daring to cross me. Fucker has no idea who he's messing with. By the time I'm done with him, he'll be lucky if he still has two rubles to rub together.

*Nobody steals from me and gets away with it. Nobody.*

My fist clenches, knuckles cracking. I allow myself a small, cruel smile.

Time to end this.

That dumbass. He's getting crushed because I'm playing the game smarter—hacking the trend, using crypto and the open market like a pro. Thanks to my slick moves in cyberspace, all his territory, supplies, and clients are jumping ship to me. It's a safer bet with me, and he knows it.

"We know their shifts, their numbers, and now their faces. At five in the morning, they'll be sluggish. That's when we fucking strike," I declare, my gaze fixed on Misha across the table. The knife he's flipping adds a rhythmic undertone to the tension filling the room. He thrives in moments like this, ready to jump into the fray.

"Yes, boss. Our men are ready to kill," Misha responds, his grin sharp, eyes alight with the thrill of the impending challenge.

I nod, my attention shifting to the photos in my hand. They're grainy, taken from a distance, but clear enough. Ivan's men, twenty-three in total, clustered around a shipment at the docks.

Each one armed, their postures relaxed but ready—a false sense of security they've draped around themselves like a cloak. I study their faces, memorize their stances.

"Vasiliev, that fucker, believes he's untouchable with his pack of rats guarding him," I spit out with disdain.

Misha leans in, peering at the photos over the expanse of the table. "Underestimating us."

"Exactly." I toss the photos down, my mind racing through scenarios. "*Pizda.*"

Surveying the room, my eyes meet those of my finest men. Warriors who've stood by me since the beginning. Without these loyal soldiers, Morozov Bratva would crumble.

Their attire speaks volumes of readiness: black tactical gear, vests bristling with ammo, faces set in determination. Misha's rallied fifteen, each one a testament to our strength.

"We hit the docks hard and fast. No mercy. We take back what's ours," I declare. A unified roar of agreement fills the room.

"Get the transport ready," I command Boris, catching his gold-haired silhouette nodding back. Quiet yet deadly, he's a force to be reckoned with.

Everyone starts to clear out, ready for the night's mission. But Misha hesitates at the door, turning back to me with a serious look. "Are you sure you want to come with us, boss?" His beard, a few days' growth, gives him a rugged edge.

"Of course." My tone leaves no room for argument.

"But the wedding…."

"For fuck's sake, Misha," I growl, frustration building. I start checking my gun, making sure it's loaded and ready. "I will not have people thinking I'm a weaker man just because I'm about to get married. This is *Bratva*, Misha. It fucking means brotherhood. I'm not ruling like some dictator. Every man here is my brother."

Misha frowns, clearly concerned. "But something may happen."

His words trail off, and for a moment, my mind wanders to Laura—her large amber eyes, the innocence that seems to wrap around her like a veil. The way she moves, speaks… it stirs something unexpected in me. A distraction I can't afford right now, not with what's at stake.

I run a hand over my face, trying to shake off the softness creeping into my thoughts. "*Blyad*," I curse under my breath.

This is not me. I'm not supposed to feel this… weakness.

"No!" I snap, sharper than I intended. "I'm going in, and I'm taking back every damn thing they stole from me."

We park the SUV in the shadows, further in where the night swallows us whole. A prickle of unease worms through me, but I shove it down deep. This is no place for doubt.

We step out into the biting cold, the river's chill wind cutting through even the toughest layers. My men, faces masked and eyes sharp, wait for my signal.

We move as one toward the dock, silent ghosts in a world of shadow and frost. Vasiliev's goons are easy to spot, huddled together for warmth, cigarettes glowing like fireflies in the dark.

"So fucking cold," one of them grumbles, wrapped in a thick hoodie that's no match for the night's bite.

"Stop complaining, dickhead," another snaps back, the smoke from his cigarette curling into the air, a fleeting serpent in the cold.

"This is fucking bullshit! What the hell are we doing here?" the first guy spits out. "I'd rather be at Tally's bar, pounding my cock into those fresh sluts."

"Fuck, yeah," one goon smirks. "Heard the next shipment's from Moldova. They have some sweet tight cunts."

"There's no tomorrow for you," I mutter under my breath.

Misha catches my eye, a silent understanding passing between us. With a subtle nod, our men spring into action. They're on the two complainers in a heartbeat, one choked silent with a wire, swift and merciless. Misha, ever the shadow, silences the other with a clean slice across the throat.

No noise, no struggle, just the end.

Quickly, efficiently, we drag their bodies into a dark alley, out of sight. Our group advances, closing in on the abandoned warehouse, the heart of tonight's operation.

As we edge closer to the warehouse, that initial thrill starts to mix with a gnawing suspicion. Something's not right. The place is too quiet; the usual signs of guard shifts, the low murmur of voices, the scuff of boots on gravel—all missing. It's like the world's holding its breath, waiting for something to snap.

"Why are there no men by the warehouse?" I murmur to Misha, my voice a whisper against the cold night air.

He shrugs, eyes scanning the darkness. "Maybe Ivan's got them all inside? Or…"

"Or it's a trap," I finish for him, the words tasting like bile in my throat. My hand instinctively tightens around my gun, the metal cold and reassuring against my skin.

We pause, reassessing. My men look to me, waiting for a decision. Every instinct screams that we're walking into a setup, yet turning back isn't an option. Not when we're this close.

"Spread out. Quietly," I order, my voice low but firm. "Check the perimeter. Something's off."

As they fan out, I take a moment to center myself. The lack of guards could mean a number of things—overconfidence on Vasiliev's part, a strategic move to draw us in, or simply a change in tactics. None of which bode well for us.

The silence is oppressive, the only sound the soft lapping of water against the dock and the distant call of a night bird. It's unnatural, this quiet, as if even the river knows to tread lightly tonight.

I can't shake the feeling that we're being watched, that Ivan's somewhere out there, smirking in the shadows. "Played us like a damn fiddle, hasn't he?" I mutter under my breath, a flash of anger cutting through the unease.

Misha, his face grim under the dim light, shakes his head. "No one. It's like they vanished into thin air."

Vanished or waiting—the thought gnaws at me. Out here, every moment we're not moving, we're vulnerable.

"Inside, then," I command, voice low. "But stay sharp."

Ignoring the knot in my stomach, we press forward. The warehouse door looms before us, open just a crack—a silent invitation or a taunt?

"Boss," Misha's hand on my arm halts me, "let's retreat; this doesn't look right."

I pause. "Fuck." My eyes scan the dark interior, then dart upwards. "Move out now," I snap, but it's too late.

Shadows detach from the rooftop, forms becoming clear. An ambush.

Gunfire erupts, a chaotic symphony of shouts and screams, the air punctuated with staccato bursts of Russian curses.

"*Pizdets!*" one of my men yells as bullets fly.

"*Suka!*" We've been played.

# Chapter 32

*Victor*

**CHAOS REIGNS** as bullets rip through the night. We're sitting ducks, caught in the open with nowhere to run. Misha's beside me, firing back with a snarl on his face.

"We need to get the fuck out of here!" he yells.

I nod, my heart pounding in my chest.

*Fuck! This was supposed to be a simple takedown, but Ivan's outplayed us.*

"Ari!" I shout over the gunfire. "Cover us!"

Ari, the giant, grunts in response, his massive frame shielding us as he returns fire.

"*Mudak*!" he curses, his voice booming over the chaos. "I'll make them pay for this!"

"*Pizdets*!" I turn to look at Igor, who's pinned down behind a crate, blood seeping from a wound in his shoulder. "Boss, we're outnumbered!"

He's right. We're outnumbered and outgunned. I signal to Misha, and he nods, understanding without words.

"Igor, you good?" I shout through the fire.

Igor, ever the stoic bastard, just grunts and nods, firing off a shot that takes down one of the shooters on the rooftop.

"I'll live. Focus on getting us the fuck out of here!"

"Smoke out on three," I yell. "One, two, three!"

Smoke grenades fly, filling the air with a thick haze. We move as one, darting through the confusion toward our waiting SUVs. Bullets whiz past, far too close for comfort.

"Sideways, move!" I bark, pushing through to Misha.

Misha nods, and we lay down a barrage, giving Ari and the others a chance to pull back. Bullets hiss past, close enough to singe. Igor's already at the SUV, engine roaring to life, his hand stretched out for me and Misha.

We bolt, dodging gunfire, debris flying everywhere. Ari's right behind, but a sudden explosion to our left sends him and Igor careening off in a different direction.

"Fuck!" The word is ripped from my throat as we split up, the plan shattered in an instant. "Go, go, go!"

Misha and I dive into the nearest SUV, tires squealing as we tear away from the warehouse, the enemy hot on our heels. Igor and Ari are a separate problem now—survival's the only game.

The SUV jolts and swerves as I take a sharp turn, nearly sending us into a spin. "Fuck, they're gaining on us!" I yell, my knuckles white on the wheel.

Misha twists in his seat, his gun already in hand. "Keep driving, boss," he growls, rolling down the window. "I'll take care of these *svolochi*."

The cold night air whips at his face as Misha leans out, taking aim at our pursuers. The first shot shatters their windshield; the second takes out a tire. The car veers off the road, flipping into a ditch with a sickening crunch of metal.

But there's no time to celebrate. More headlights appear in the distance, a relentless swarm of death and vengeance. We're not out of the woods yet, not by a long shot.

The streets blur into a frenzied streak of lights and shadows as we weave through the city, Ivan Vasiliev's men relentless. They knew; somehow, they knew exactly when and where to hit us.

The chase is on, a deadly game of cat and mouse through the city streets. I drive like a madman, taking corners on two wheels, trying to lose our tail. But they're good, matching us move for move.

"They're closing in, boss!" Misha shouts, his eyes fixed on the rearview mirror.

I glance back, see the glare of headlights growing larger, the sound of gunfire echoing in the night. "Not for long," I growl, my grip tightening on the wheel.

A sharp turn onto a less traveled road offers a brief respite, but it's a fleeting victory. The enemy's SUVs are relentless, bullets peppering the back of our vehicle, glass shattering, metal screaming.

"We can't keep this up forever," Misha says, his voice tense. "We need a plan."

"I'm working on it," I snap, my mind racing. "Just keep them off our ass!"

Misha nods, leaning out the window and firing back at our pursuers. The sound of gunfire fills the air, mixed with the roar of the engine and the pounding of my heart.

Igor takes the lead, his SUV tearing down the road like a bat out of hell. Ari's right behind him, his massive frame barely fitting behind the wheel.

"Come on, you bastards," I mutter under my breath. "Just a little longer."

But Ivan's men are like a pack of wolves, hungry for blood. They swarm around us, trying to force us off the road, to trap us in a web of steel and fire.

"Damnit, they're everywhere!" Misha shouts, ducking back inside as a bullet whizzes past his head.

I grit my teeth, swerving to avoid a hail of gunfire. "We've got to shake them, now!" An unexpected pothole sends us veering, the vehicle barely under control. "Hold on!" I shout as we skid, the world tilting wildly. In the chaos, a plan forms—risky, insane, but it's all we've got.

I floor it, the engine roaring as we push the limits of speed and control. Bullets crack the rear window, sending shards of glass flying.

Up ahead, Igor swerves to avoid a hail of gunfire, his vehicle careening off the road and into the darkness.

"*Blyad*!" I curse, my heart sinking. We can't stop, can't turn back.

Ari's SUV is next, a well-aimed shot taking out his tires. He spins out, crashing into a ditch with a sickening crunch of metal.

I take a quick peek at Ari, my heart in my throat. He's alive, crawling out of the wreckage with a look of pure fury on his face. He catches my eye, nods once, then turns his attention to the two vehicles now solely focused on us.

It's clear now—Ivan's men have one target in mind, and that's me.

They want me dead, no matter the cost.

It's just us now, Misha and me, hurtling down the road with Ivan's men hot on our heels. "We need to lose them!" Misha yells, leaning out the window to return fire.

"I'm open to suggestions!" I shout back, my mind racing.

A sudden movement catches my eye. Misha lunges across the seat, his body slamming into mine. The crack of a gunshot splits the air, and Misha grunts in pain, his shoulder jerking back. Blood blooms across his shirt, but his eyes are fierce, focused.

"Misha, what the fuck!" I yell, realizing what he's done. He's taken a bullet for me, the crazy bastard.

"Just drive," he grits out, his hand pressed against the wound. "I'll live."

I floor the accelerator, my heart pounding. Misha's blood is on my hands, literally and figuratively. I've got to get us out of this, got to make sure his sacrifice isn't in vain.

I grit my teeth, my mind racing. We're running out of road and options. Up ahead, a narrow bridge looms, the river churning below.

"Hold on," I growl, my foot pressing the pedal to the floor. Misha braces himself, his eyes wide as he realizes my plan.

The SUV leaps forward, tires screeching as we hurtle toward the bridge. Ivan's men are right behind us, their headlights blinding in the rearview.

At the last second, I jerk the wheel, sending us crashing through the guardrail. For a moment, we're airborne, the world suspended in breathless anticipation.

Then we're falling, plunging toward the icy depths below. "*Yob tvoyu mat'*!" Misha screams, his voice lost in the roar of the wind and the rush of the river.

We hit the water hard, the impact slamming us forward. Everything goes black, the cold and the chaos swallowing us whole.

The icy water shocks me back to consciousness, its frigid grip threatening to pull me under. I gasp for air, my lungs burning as I struggle to the surface. Beside me, Misha thrashes, his face contorted in pain.

"Misha!" I yell, my voice raw and desperate. I grab him by the collar, hauling him toward the shore with every ounce of strength I have left. He's dead weight in my arms, his blood mixing with the churning water.

We collapse on the riverbank, gasping and shivering. Misha's eyes flutter open, glazed with pain. "Boss," he croaks, his hand pressed against his side. Blood seeps between his fingers, stark against his pale skin.

"Hang on," I growl, tearing off my jacket to staunch the flow. "We're getting out of this."

But even as I say it, I hear the screeching of tires, the shouts of Ivan's men. They've found us.

I drag Misha behind the wrecked SUV, my heart pounding in my chest. He's fading fast, his breath coming in short, sharp gasps.

I press the fabric against his wound, my hands shaking. He's losing too much blood, his face growing paler by the second.

"You shouldn't have done that," I say, my voice rough with emotion. "Taking that bullet… you could've died."

Misha laughs, a wet, gurgling sound. "And let you have all the fun? Not a chance."

I shake my head, a mix of gratitude and frustration welling up inside me. This is the kind of loyalty that can't be bought, the kind that runs deeper than blood.

And I'll be damned if I let him die on me now.

"Don't you fucking die on me tonight," I yell. As I peer around the twisted metal, my stomach dropping at the sight of Ivan's men surrounding us. They're closing in, their guns drawn and ready.

For a moment, I close my eyes, Laura's face flashing before me. Her smile, her laugh, the way she looks at me like I'm the only man in the world.

*No. I can't die here. Not like this. Not when I have so much to live for.*

I grit my teeth, loading my gun with steady hands. "I'm getting married today," I mutter, more to myself than to Misha. "And no fucking *mudak* is going to stop me."

Misha laughs, a wet, gurgling sound that turns into a cough. "Give 'em hell, boss," he rasps, his eyes glinting with fierce pride.

I nod, my jaw set.

I burst from cover, firing with deadly precision.

One, two, three men drop, their bodies crumpling to the ground.

But they keep coming, bullets whizzing past my head, biting into the metal at my back. I'm running out of time, out of options.

Misha's still firing, his aim true even as his life bleeds out onto the frozen ground. "*Suka blyad!*" he roars, taking down two more before his gun clicks empty.

I'm down to my last clip, my last chance. Ivan's men are almost on us, their shadows looming like death itself.

And then I hear it—the roar of engines, the screech of tires. Headlights pierce the darkness, blinding in their intensity.

This is it, I think, my heart thundering. This is how it ends.

But I'll be damned if I go down without a fight. Without giving these *mudaks* a taste of their own medicine.

I look at Misha, my brother-in-arms, my loyal friend. He meets my gaze, a silent understanding passing between us. We both know the odds are stacked against us, that this might be our last stand.

But we're Bratva. We don't surrender, we don't back down. We fight until our last breath, until our bones are dust and our blood runs cold.

I take a deep breath, Laura's face burning bright in my mind.

*She's waiting for me, counting on me to come back to her.*

And I will. I'm going back to Laura, even if I have to crawl out of my own grave to do it.

I grip my gun tighter, my finger hovering over the trigger.

"*Ya ne sdalus' bez boya,*" I mutter, the words like steel on my tongue. "I won't go down without a fight."

Misha grins, a feral, bloodstained thing. "*Da*, boss. Let's give 'em hell."

# Chapter 33

*Laura*

**I KNOW** he's there even before I see him.

My body tenses up, all instincts on alert for trouble.

As I come to, the room's dark and I'm not by myself.

My heart thumps loudly in my chest as I take in the figure standing by the bed.

*Victor.*

He stands tall and foreboding, a dark silhouette against the dim nightlight. His piercing gaze never wavers from me as he looms over the bed, naked, every defined muscle on his bare chest is glistening with sweat and ready for action.

A shiver runs through my body as my nipples harden under the soft cashmere robe, aching for his touch.

"Victor," I gasp, feeling exposed and vulnerable in just my flimsy panties and robe on top of the sheets. He stands there, silent and unmoving, but I can see the raw desire burning in his eyes.

"Why… why are you here?"

He stays quiet.

I feel the bed dip under his weight as he climbs in. I sense his entire body charged with an electric current that sends sparks shooting through me. My heart races as he hovers over me.

"I wanted you to stay, just stay with me…" I blurt out, surprised at my own words.

"I'm here now *kiska*," he murmurs, his voice deep and low, his lips curl into a sinister smile, his eyes blazing with an intense hunger.

Trembling with anticipation, I reach out to touch him but stop when he leans over me, planting a hand by my head and gripping my neck. His fingers wrap tightly around my throat. I gasp for air, the pressure of his grip both exhilarating and terrifying.

His other hand grips my breast, sending waves of pain and pleasure coursing through me. His fingers twist and squeeze my aching nipple.

"Oh, God!"

"Oh, my God!"

"Yes…Victor."

Every nerve in my body is alight as I struggle between wanting to break free and surrendering to his dominance.

His hands glide down my body, tracing a path to my belly button before spreading my legs wide open and sliding my panties aside. My heart races with excitement and anticipation as he plunges his fingers into my soaking wet pussy.

I never thought I'd get turned on by such a dangerous and forbidden situation, but the thrill only adds to the intensity. My hand instinctively reaches for his throbbing cock. It's too big for my fingers to fully encircle, but I grip it tightly and eagerly stroke it as our bodies move in perfect rhythm.

"Fuck," he groans with primal need, "you're so fucking wet for me, *kiska*."

"Ahh... you are insatiable." I lick my lips greedily as I continue to stroke him, feeling his hardened length pulsating beneath my touch. My breath quickens, and my heart races as I succumb to the primal desire coursing through my veins. My stroke grows more desperate as he lets out a growl, sounding almost like an animal.

His fingers curl deeper and harder inside me, driving me wild with desire and ecstasy. A sharp gasp escapes my lips as I'm overwhelmed with pleasure, followed by a desperate moan that echoes through the room. I curse under my breath, unable to contain the overwhelming rush of passion coursing through my body.

"More," I beg breathlessly, unable to hold back any longer as the intensity continues to build. My body trembles with anticipation and longing for what's to come next.

His rough fingers, slick with my arousal, slide effortlessly over my throbbing clit. I moan in pleasure as he teases me through the fabric of my damp panties.

"You like that, don't you, *kiska*?" he growls in my ear.

Before I can respond, his lips crash onto mine, hungrily devouring me. I greedily taste him as he nibbles on my lip, his hands roaming over my body and setting every nerve alight.

With one swift movement, he removes my panties, and my robe falls to the floor. His hands are rough and demanding as they roam all over my exposed skin. He bites down on each of my nipples, sending waves of pleasurable pain through my body.

"Spread your legs for me," he demands, and I eagerly comply. "Let me fuck you," he grunts in a low voice. "I'll fuck you hard."

I nod desperately, unable to form words as he enters me with force.

With a fierce grunt, he thrusts into me, gripping my breasts in his hands and using them as leverage. His movements are wild and unrelenting, driving me to the edge of ecstasy. I cling onto his shoulders desperately, afraid of flying off and crashing into the headboard.

His eyes blaze with an intense passion that almost frightens me. But I can't look away, even as I feel another surge building inside me.

I clench my pussy around his pulsating hard cock, feeling every inch of him throb inside of me. My body shudders with the intense pleasure as I squeeze him tightly, begging for more and pushing him deeper.

"Fuck, yes!"

"Yes!"

I've never felt such an intense craving.

"You'll come again for me," he growls, triumphant. "Your slutty little cunt craves nothing more than being filled by its master's cock." My pussy grips onto him as if I never want to let go. The sound of our skin slapping together echoes around us.

"Fuck, yes!" I scream, overcome with pleasure as another orgasm consumes me. But my pleasure is suddenly cut short by a deafening gunshot that cracks through the air. The sound of dark laughter follows, mocking me as I am consumed by waves of fear and confusion.

Victor's weight suddenly crushes me, his body unnaturally still. A cold dampness spreads across my hair and skin.

Panicked, I push him, my voice trembling as I cry, "Victor? Victor, wake up!" But he's unresponsive, heavy. The dark stain on my shoulder and hair sends my heart into a frenzy.

With a desperate shove, I manage to roll him off.

My eyes are met with horror—a bullet hole in his forehead, blood a stark contrast against his skin.

Trembling uncontrollably, I bring my bloodstained hands to my mouth, tasting the metallic tang of death.

Tears blur my vision as I whisper in disbelief, "No, this can't be happening."

---

Rolling the diamond ring on my finger does nothing to ease the knot in my chest. I catch the time on the clock by the bed—it's six in the morning already.

The night was rough, my nightmares worse than any before. Victor's face messed up in my dreams. A bullet right through his head, turning those sharp gray eyes pitch black, like the life in them just vanished.

A chill ripples through me as I sit up, trying to shake off the dread.

"Could he be dead?" I murmur to myself, my heart thudding painfully at the thought. It's a weird ache, deep and sharp.

*Laur, get a grip.*

Rubbing my chest, I try to ease the tightness, to shake off the cold dread that's settled there.

There's no way I can fall back asleep now.

I slide out of bed, the silk nightgown feeling out of place on my skin. It's a constant reminder that my life has taken a surreal turn. The luxury around me feels empty, meaningless.

Anxiety won't let me sit still. I pace the room, trying to shake off the unease.

"It was just a nightmare," I tell myself, hoping to believe it.

But the truth nags at me. Victor is in the mafia, a world steeped in danger and death. Why does the thought of him hurt like this? He's the reason I'm trapped in this golden cage. Yet, the worry for him feels as real as the grief I felt for my mom, lost to her sorrows.

*Fuck, I'm overthinking again.*

I force myself to stop pacing, realizing I need a distraction, something to cleanse the remnants of the nightmare clinging to my mind.

The idea of a shower flickers through my thoughts like a beacon. Maybe the water can wash away the images, the fear.

As the silk of my nightgown slides over my head and falls to the floor, the chill of the room brushes against my skin, a stark contrast to the warmth I'm about to seek. I step into the shower, letting the water cascade over me. But it does little to wash away the dread.

My heart feels heavy. "I'll go look for him," I consider.

*No, Laur. He's not your husband; he's your captor!*

*Decision made. I won't go searching for him.*

Finishing the shower, I wrap a fluffy towel around myself, almost in a hug, seeking comfort from its soft embrace.

I approach the fogged mirror, wiping it with a hand to clear my reflection. It's then I notice the puffiness around my eyes.

"Did I cry?" I murmur, staring at the stranger in the mirror.

The realization hits harder than the cold tiles beneath my feet. I've been shaken to my core by a nightmare, by the possibility of a loss I hadn't even admitted mattered to me. This concern for Victor... it's unsettling, confusing.

*Why the hell do I care so much?*

I take a deep breath, trying to anchor myself to the here and now.

I wander into the walk-in closet.

*A fucking walk-in closet.*

The realization that I now have a "his and hers" closet hits me hard. The dresses, all organized by color, the suits, and the extravagant pieces—it's all too much.

Running my fingers over the fabrics, sequins, and lace, all this luxury still feels alien to me.

I puff out my cheeks in frustration, scanning the closet filled with outfits that scream wealth. No jeans in sight, just dresses and pants too fancy for my taste.

I really miss my own clothes. They might be nothing fancy, just sweatshirts and long pants, but they're *me.*

In the end, I opt for the least extravagant pair of black pants and a simple, though clearly designer, white blouse.

Slipping on a pair of sneakers that fit perfectly, I can't help but be impressed. "Wow, they've got everything down, from my underwear to my shoe size."

Glancing at the ring on my finger, I realize… "This, too." It must be the same size that Victor's mom wore.

Approaching a full-length mirror, a silent curse escapes me.

"Shit, I look… elegant." There's a moment of disbelief as I see myself looking like those rich wives from Beverly Hills, a world away from my own reality.

The vastness of my room—or should I call it a suite?—hits me again. It dwarfs my old apartment, turning my past life into a distant memory.

*What do I do now?*

I let out a long sigh.

*One breath at a time. Laur, just be thankful you're still breathing today.*

Determined to shake off my restlessness, I make my way downstairs.

The house is waking up; the soft morning light filters through grand windows, casting shadows that dance on the walls.

The early morning light casting a soft glow through the grand space. The TV remote sits precisely where it's supposed to be on the coffee table. I sink into the plush sofa and try the TV, but nothing holds my interest. It's too early, and my mind is elsewhere.

I shut it off, realizing it's still early, just half past six.

"Fine, I'll go look for him." I finally give in to the worry gnawing at me.

*Damn, why does the nightmare bother me so much?*

He's the man who took me from my life.

Without realizing it, my feet carry me to the door, half thinking it'll be locked. But it opens right up.

"Oh! Did they forget to lock me in?" Stepping out, I move quietly, almost like a thief, down the corridor, recalling Victor's words about his meeting room.

"Maybe he's there, working? Or maybe dealing with mafia stuff…"

The corridors feel endless, lined with doors that hide secrets and stories I can only guess at.

I notice the voices of maids downstairs as I approach a room, the door slightly open, light spilling out. Nearing it, I freeze at the sound of Ksenia's voice, tense and low, her frustration barely contained.

"What the fuck happened there, Igor?" she snaps into the phone.

My steps betray me, pulling me toward the door.

Logic yells at me to back off, to keep out of mafia messes. Yet, here I am, curiosity bulldozing my caution.

"What do you mean you guys got ambushed?" Ksenia's voice slices through the silence, sharp and demanding.

I edge closer, making sure to stay out of sight, holding my breath like it could make me invisible. Peeking around the corner, I see Ksenia in full force.

She's there, in the heart of Victor's dark, wood-drenched office, chaos in the form of papers and files strewn across the desk. Ksenia leans over them, glasses perched on her nose, phone clutched tight. The air smells of old books and something… richer, darker.

I barely breathe, watching Ksenia handle the crisis on the phone.

She paces back and forth, her hand gripping the phone tight enough to make her knuckles white. Every so often, she stops, pinches the bridge of her nose like she's fighting off a headache or trying to squeeze the bad news into something manageable.

With a long slow breath, her next question answers every piece of dread from my nightmare.

"Tell me now, is Victor *dead*?"

**Victor and Laura's journey continues with a promise of their happily ever after in *'Velvet Chains,'* Book 2 of the Bond by Morozov Bratva series.**

https://www.amazon.com/dp/B0D3T5YNHH

Can You Drop a Review on **AMAZON**?

https://www.amazon.com/product-review/B0CZWTQGMC

I'd love to hear your thoughts!

*Want more steamy mafia romance?*

Follow my author page to stay in the loop!

### AMAZON

https://www.amazon.com/Mya-Grey/e/B0874LH9CN

### GOODREADS

https://www.goodreads.com/author/show/20249010.Mya_Grey

### BOOKBUB

https://www.bookbub.com/authors/mya-grey-c6b5463a-f6c8-49e7-a0ea-1ce28f496f76

Let's keep the conversation going! Follow me on social media for more fun and engaging content.

### FACEBOOK

https://www.facebook.com/author.myagrey/

### YOUTUBE

https://www.youtube.com/channel/UCP932MIra_hRsNZT1oHpYLQ

### TIKTOK

https://www.tiktok.com/@myagreywriteslove?is_from_webapp=1&sender_device=pc

Printed in Great Britain
by Amazon